Lattes and Larceny

NOLA ROBERTSON

ISBN: 978-1-953213-27-3

CHAPTER ONE

It was difficult to breathe and maintain an enjoyable state of slumber with a heavy weight pressing down on my chest. The periodic paw thwacks to my chin weren't helping either, and I was forced to open my eyes and find Luna, Aunt Delia's cat, staring down at me.

I liked animals of the pet variety, but this particular one, a Persian with long white hair and a brown mask around her blue eyes, had a haughty personality and didn't warm up to people easily. The last time I'd seen her, we'd developed a semi-cordial relationship. That had been several years ago, so I guessed in her mind I was an intruder, which explained why she was intent on annoying me until I got out of bed.

"Hey, Luna," I cooed. When my friendly attempt to reconnect didn't soften her glare or stop her from raising a paw, I shifted onto my side and forced her to move before she could resort to using claws.

A rap on the door was followed by Delia peeking her head into the room. "Brinley, are you awake?"

I smiled at the face whose rounded cheeks and pert nose closely resembled my own. Except for my light brown hair and hazel eyes, I looked more like my aunt

1

than I did my mother, who was also her sister. Delia's blue eyes and dark hair, intermingled with silver, were her only contrasting features.

Like me, Delia was an early riser. The drive to her place had taken almost four hours, and that was after putting in over eight long and arduous hours at work. If I hadn't arrived late and been exhausted, I would've already been out of bed.

"I am now… Thanks to Luna," I said, sitting up and crossing my legs under the covers. The cat hadn't moved from the bed. I raised my hand to pet her, then thought better of it when she crouched lower and looked as if she might reward my efforts with an attack.

"Sorry about that," Delia said, stepping into the room. "She recently figured out how to open doors."

The guest room door had a brass handle instead of a knob, and I could easily picture Luna jumping up and pulling it down. Even before Delia mentioned it, I'd wondered how the cat had gotten into the room. At first, I thought I'd imagined closing the door before going to bed the night before. Cats were intelligent and resilient creatures, this one more than most, so I wasn't surprised to hear about her latest achievement.

My aunt loved her pet, but she never pretended to believe the cat possessed any angelic qualities. Delia lifted Luna off the bed and set her on the floor. "Go on, you naughty girl."

Miffed by her owner's scolding, the cat raised her tail, padded across the carpet, then slipped into the hallway.

"I'm thrilled to have you here," Delia said, taking a seat on the edge of the bed next to me. "But I get the feeling there's more to your visit than coming to see my new place."

My travel plans had been impulsive ones, not something I ever did. I was organized, a planner, which had earned me a decent job in the marketing department of a large firm.

After receiving some life-altering news at work, I needed some advice that didn't come from any of my co-workers. Leaving the city where I currently lived and going home to the town I'd grown up in would've been my first choice.

I enjoyed spending time with my father. The man had an easy-going personality, which was a complete opposite to my mother's stringent, must-keep-up-social-appearances persona. Rather than enduring her views on what she thought I should do, which never coincided with what I truly wanted, I decided to forgo an unpleasant argument and take Delia up on her invitation to spend time with her instead. An invitation she'd managed to work into every conversation we'd had since she'd moved to Hawkins Harbor.

As far as relatives went, my aunt had given me a much-needed parental role throughout my life. When asked, she would also provide valuable insight. The significant difference between her and my mother was letting me decide whether or not I wanted to implement the advice.

When things had gone wrong at work, Delia was the first person I called to talk about it. I hadn't given her all the details at the time but had gotten the support I needed anyway. "Do you remember me telling you that my boss was getting ready to retire, and he was training me to take over his position?" I asked. I'd been co-managing an entire department and had spent the last six months learning everything I could and working my backside off so I'd be ready by the time he left.

"I do," Delia said, shifting and placing one leg with knee bent on the bed to face me. "It's the reason you couldn't take time off to visit." There was understanding in her tone, not the chastising barbs I would've received from my mother. I felt a pang of guilt about not coming to see her sooner and wished I hadn't let my ambition get in the way.

Delia furrowed her brow. "After all your hard work,

did they decide not to promote you after all?"

I played with a portion of comforter stretched across my lap, the disappointing pressure I'd been experiencing for days returning to my chest. "I got the promotion, just not the one I'd expected."

"But it's still good news, right?" Delia asked, trying to sound encouraging.

"No," I said, shaking my head. "They want to ship me off to their Minneapolis branch." Living hours away from my family was one thing, but taking up residence several states away was another.

Business-related trips had taken me to the beautiful northern city on several occasions, once during the coldest time of the year. The residents had adapted to the winter weather. Some of them seemed to enjoy it, but I hadn't. Thinking about the frigid temperatures and not feeling entirely warm during my stay made me shiver.

I'd been born and raised in Florida. Sunshine, palm trees, and the occasional trip to the beach so I could feel the sand between my toes, was a way of life. Months of cold weather and learning how to wield a snow shovel bigger than the one I'd used to build sand castles as a child didn't sound appealing.

I wasn't prone to crying but knew if I let my frustration get the better of me, the tears were going to fall…again.

"What? Did they tell you why?" Delia asked, not bothering to hide her outrage.

"My boss said he didn't know, but I got the impression he did and wasn't allowed to tell me the real reason."

Delia flashed me a weak smile. "And knowing you, I expect that you dug around until you got an answer."

"I did." It helped to have a good rapport with the assistants who worked for the high-ranking executives in the company. For the price of a lunch, I'd learned who had sabotaged my career. The why hadn't been hard to figure out once I discovered the name of the person responsible.

"And," Delia said when I took too long to explain.

"It was because of Stacy Adler, the CEO's daughter and the current girlfriend of a guy I used to date," I said a little more sarcastically than I'd meant to.

"You haven't mentioned dating anyone in a while," Delia said. "Are you talking about that guy you worked with?" She tapped her chin. "What was his name?"

"Rick."

"So, what happened?" Delia asked.

"From what I understand, Stacy is possessive of the guys she dates," I said. "Word has it that she and Rick are pretty serious. Apparently, she got upset when she found out that he and I had dated and said something to her father that got me transferred out of state."

Though why our past relationship bothered her still baffled me. Inter-office dating was usually frowned upon because it rarely ended well, but it had been different in my case. Rick and I had gone out for a couple of months shortly after I'd started working for the company. We'd kept things casual, nothing that involved a noticeable romantic involvement or a commitment.

When we'd parted ways, we'd remained friends, or at least friendly, since we worked in separate departments and on different floors in the same building. Now, the only time we saw each other was at company events or a chance meeting in the lobby or elevator.

"Well, that's just wrong," Delia said, crossing her arms.

"Tell me about it," I said. If I didn't like the company and most of the people I worked with, giving notice and choosing a new career path would've been an easy decision. All businesses had employees and executives that were difficult to deal with, but as a whole, the company I worked for only had a handful. I couldn't complain about the people I'd interacted with in the Minnesota office either. They'd all been pleasant and willing to make my job less stressful.

Even with my aversion to living in a colder climate, I might have been more receptive to the transfer if I'd been given a choice, not had it made for me based on jealousy and familial nepotism.

"Can't you tell them no and at least stay in your current position?" Delia asked.

As angry as I'd been, and as much as I wanted the promotion, I'd considered the option. "They've already found a person to take my place," I said, slumping my shoulders.

"When do they expect you to start your new job?" Delia asked, still trying to be supportive yet unable to mask the disappointment in her voice.

"They've given me three weeks, not counting the one I'm spending here, to make all the arrangements."

"Then let's not waste a minute of it," Delia said, patting my leg, then rising from the bed.

My aunt had an adventurous nature and could be quite resilient when faced with adversity. They were qualities I greatly admired. She'd taken the settlement money she'd received after divorcing Craig Danton, my uncle by marriage, and used a portion of it to buy her home. At the time, I'd understood her need to start a new life, but I wasn't sure why she'd chosen this town out of all the ones located along the coast.

With an entire week to spend relaxing, shopping, and doing whatever I wanted, I was certain I'd have my answer by the time I left to go home. I sighed, knowing that home was a term that wouldn't apply to the apartment I'd rented for very much longer. Not with the short amount of time I had left before my relocation became a reality. Returning to the city was a depressing prospect, one I hoped my vacation would help me ignore.

"Instead of having breakfast here, I thought we'd walk over to the Flavored Bean so I can introduce you to my friends Myrna and Vincent," Delia said. "Archer, the owner, has quite a selection of coffees, and I guarantee you won't be disappointed."

It was hard not to be affected by my aunt's enthusiasm.

I pushed back the comforter and got out of bed. "As long as there's food with the coffee, I'm in."

CHAPTER TWO

After treating myself to a long shower and getting dressed, I was ready to face the first day of my vacation. Hopefully, Delia's itinerary would keep me so busy that I wouldn't have time to worry about the unwanted direction my career had taken.

After making a quick stop to see if she'd returned to her bedroom and finding it empty, I headed downstairs. Delia was waiting for me in the kitchen. "Thanks again for letting me stay with you," I said as I crossed the room and gave her a hug, holding on a few seconds longer than necessary. I had no idea when I'd be able to visit her again, and silly as it was, I wanted to stock up for the future and make up for the hugs I'd missed since she'd moved.

She held me at arm's length. "Should you decide Minnesota isn't right for you, then I want you to know that you are welcome to stay here for as long as you want."

"Thanks, I appreciate the offer. I'm sure I'll be fine," I said, even though for the first time in ages, an unease of doubt surged through me. I'd gotten my first job at the age of sixteen and had been self-sufficient ever since. No matter how much I would miss her, taking handouts from my aunt didn't bode well with me.

"Of course, you will," Delia said, releasing me and taking a step back. "Are you ready to go?" After attaching a cobalt blue fanny pack to her hip, she held out an arm urging me toward the living room.

I was starving and looking forward to one of Archer's special brews, so coercing of any kind hadn't been necessary. Smiling, I grabbed my purse off the chair where I'd left it the night before, then pulled the strap over my shoulder as I followed my aunt out the front door.

Feeling the sunshine on my face as I stepped off the porch brightened my day, and I could feel some of the stress easing from my body. Delia had a double-car garage, and I assumed that's where she kept her vehicle. My car was sitting in the driveway and more accessible, so I dug through my purse, searching for my keys.

"You won't need those." Delia flicked her wrist. "Pretty much everything is close by, so I hope you don't mind walking."

It was troubling to realize that any walking I'd done back home was rushed and usually work-related. I couldn't remember the last time I'd taken a leisurely stroll on purpose and was looking forward to it. "I don't mind at all." I dropped the keys in my bag and followed her to the sidewalk running parallel to the street.

Other than the areas lit by occasional street light, the neighborhood had been dark when I'd arrived the night before. I stopped, taking a moment to look around and enjoy the view.

Most of the houses were trimmed in white, and their exteriors were done in varying shades of tans, grays, or light khaki green. Most of the homes were single stories, with a random few having second floors like Delia's.

All of them had manicured green lawns, some landscaped with the occasional palm tree and flower beds.

"This is a beautiful neighborhood," I said as we strolled along the sidewalk that appeared to be taking us closer to the beach. "I can see why you moved here."

My aunt was in her late fifties and could've kept working if she'd wanted to. The money she'd set aside over the years combined with the divorce settlement was enough to provide her with a comfortable early retirement. I couldn't blame her. Who wouldn't want to enjoy a leisurely life living near the beach?

"Myrna and Vincent live in the Pelican Promenade Retirement Community, which begins on the next street over," Delia said, waving her hand in the general direction.

I'd never met my aunt's friends, but she talked about them frequently during our phone conversations, so I already knew that Myrna had never been married and Vincent was a widower. They all lived in the same neighborhood, but Delia's house was near the beach, while Myrna's and Vincent's homes were inside the retirement community.

We were about to cross the street when a white truck with turquoise waves painted across the lower half of the exterior approached us. The words "Noonan's Lawn Maintenance" with a website and telephone number were printed in black letters on the driver's door.

The driver had his window rolled down and slowed to a stop near the edge of the pavement. "Good morning," he said, placing his left arm on the frame.

"Delia, how's it going?" asked the woman who was sitting in the passenger seat as she leaned forward so we could see her.

"Great," Delia said, tugging me toward them. "I want you to meet my niece, Brinley. She's going to be staying with me for the next week."

"This is Brady Noonan and his sister Avery," Delia said once we reached the truck.

"Hey," I said, leaning forward so I could see Avery better and noticed the similarities in facial features and hair color. Their outfits were geared for a day of work; Avery wore a cotton dress and light-weight jacket, and Brady wore a tank top that clung tightly to his muscular chest. It was clear by his deep tan and lighter blond streaks that Brady spent most of his days working outside.

"Brady does the lawns for quite a few people in the area, mine included," Delia said. "Avery's the event's coordinator for the Promenade."

"I'll bet that keeps you busy," I said, reminded of the demanding managerial duties I performed via my own job.

"It's a lot of work, but I enjoy it," Avery said, smiling.

"Your efforts are greatly appreciated," Delia said, then placed her hand on my arm. "We'll have to take a look at the schedule and see if there's something you'd like to attend while you're here."

Other than spending time with my aunt, I hadn't considered doing any socializing. Now that she mentioned it, getting out and doing something different had a lot of appeal. The center was geared toward an older crowd, and I couldn't imagine my aunt participating in anything that wasn't a little exciting. "That sounds like fun," I said, striving to sound enthusiastic and hoping I hadn't just agreed to do anything mundane, like watching a chess match. I occasionally liked playing board games but lost interest in the ones that required a lot of strategic planning, which was surprising given my chosen profession.

"I look forward to seeing you again," Avery said, then glanced at her wristwatch. "We'd better get going. My boss gets upset when his employees don't show up for work on time."

Unless someone had a family emergency, most employers weren't happy when their workers didn't adhere to their assigned schedules. I certainly didn't want to be the reason Avery was late. "No problem," I said, moving away from the vehicle.

"Hawkins Harbor really is a great place to live," Delia said once we were on our way again.

I'd forgotten how breathtaking a panoramic view of the ocean and beach could be and stopped to enjoy the moment. Billowy clouds dotted the horizon. A mild breeze drifted through the air, along with the smell of brine from the ocean. Watching the gentle waves roll in, then recede, had a hypnotically calming effect.

"Over to the right, you can just make out the harbor and marina." Delia pointed as she spoke. "We get a fair amount of tourists and some who like to charter boats for day fishing. If you decide you'd like to do something spontaneous, we can always sign up for scuba lessons."

I had an aversion to visiting a playground that belonged to creatures larger than me, who also happened to have sharp teeth. The aquarium was about as close to an underwater adventure as I wanted to get.

"Or not," Delia said when she caught me wrinkling my nose. "Please tell me you're at least going to get in the water and that you remembered to bring your bathing suit."

"Are you kidding? It was one of the first things I packed," I chuckled. "I'm actually looking forward to a week of not having to wear business outfits that include skirts, pants, and heels." I glanced down at the tank top, shorts, and sandals I was wearing, then frowned at the pale skin on my arms and legs. "I plan to get in a lot of sun while I'm here."

Working overtime had become a way of life, at least for the last few months. I'd barely noticed spring's arrival, and now that it was almost over, I planned to enjoy what was left of it. Not for the first time since learning I wasn't getting the job I'd wanted, I questioned if putting my personal life on hold had been a waste of time.

I'd done quite a bit of reflecting during the drive to my aunt's place, but I'd been too exhausted and too stressed to think about things clearly. After getting a decent amount of sleep, my brain was back to functioning properly, and I wondered how long my transfer to Minnesota had been in the works. It pained me even more to think my boss may have known about it longer than he was willing to admit.

"Good, because I don't think there's anything better

than spending an afternoon on the beach to make a person feel better," Delia said.

"Except maybe some shopping," I finished with the encouraging words she'd given me numerous times over the years. My aunt was an expert shopper with an uncanny ability to find the best sales any store had to offer.

"So you have been listening to me all this time," Delia giggled, then draped an arm over my shoulder. "Speaking of shopping." She aimed me in the opposite direction, which happened to be a street cordoned off from the beach by four-foot-high cylinder posts spaced several feet apart and painted a bright blue. Posted nearby was a sign that read, "Pedestrian traffic only. No vehicles allowed."

From where we were standing, I glimpsed signs for several clothes boutiques and a souvenir store. Excitement rushed through me at the prospect of exploring all the shops on both sides of the street. A day without rushing, spent looking for sales, was something else I hadn't done in a while. "I can't wait." My stomach picked that moment to rumble.

"Maybe we should eat first," Delia said, then got us moving again.

We hadn't gone very far past the end of the road before reaching a mint green building with the words "The Flavored Bean" painted on a large wooden sign hanging over the entrance. Small town businesses were notorious for using pastel or bright colors to be more noticeable. Not that the coffee bar, a stand-alone building that appeared to be a renovated house, needed any additional features to be noticed.

There was a raised deck with round, umbrella-covered tables that faced the beach. If the roof had been thatched instead of shingled, it could've easily been mistaken for a tiki bar. With the palm trees and beach nearby, the place reminded me of something found on a tropical vacation and seemed appropriate given the fact that I'd just started mine.

Hearing my aunt's name being hollered interrupted my perusal of the place. It drew my attention to the older man and woman approaching us on the sidewalk intersecting with the one we were using.

"Hey, Myrna, Vincent," Delia called and waved.

"Good morning." Myrna enthusiastically waved back, and Vincent responded with a nod.

Myrna's short curly strands had more silver than dark brown, and with a stocky build, she couldn't be more than three inches over five feet. Vincent was much taller and had thin wisps of hair covering a balding head. If I didn't know he was a local, judging by his wardrobe choice of red floral shirt and khaki shorts, I would have assumed he was a tourist.

When the two of them got closer, I couldn't help but smile at the yellow tennis shoes and purple socks that didn't match the rest of Myrna's outfit. Neither Vincent nor my aunt seemed to notice. Maybe unusual outer wear was the older woman's thing. Like people who wore body piercings or different colored streaks in their hair.

"You must be Brinley," Myrna said as soon as she reached us. "We've heard so much about you."

I was surprised to have a stranger pull me into an overly generous hug. My family wasn't big on displays of affection, so other than my aunt, getting more than a verbal welcome was a rarity in my life. I could feel the heat rising on my cheeks when she finally released me.

Unsure how to interpret that tidbit of information, I shot Delia a sidelong glance, hoping that she hadn't shared my life story with her friends.

"Don't mind Myrna. She's a hugger," Vincent said. "You'll get used to it."

Myrna snorted and pretended like she was going to wrap her arms around him. When Vincent frowned and took a step back, she cackled and said, "Let's go in. I'm starving."

If their days were filled with these kinds of antics, I

could see why my aunt enjoyed spending time with them. I found myself relaxing even more and looking forward to our upcoming meal. As we filed one by one up the stairs and into the building, I noticed a store-bought help wanted sign taped to the door. Someone had used a black marker and filled in the words "Manager Wanted." Before I could give the sign any more thought or ask Delia questions to fulfill my curiosity, I was distracted by the enticing aroma of freshly brewed coffee and baked goodies.

CHAPTER THREE

Unlike the building's brightly colored exterior, the inside of the Flavored Bean was done in tans and dark browns, with hunter green edging the trim running along the floor and ceiling. What immediately caught my eye was the large aquarium filled with colorful fish built into the wall behind a bar lined with stools. A handful of tables, each with four chairs, sat on the hardwood floor in the middle of the room.

On the left, as my aunt's friends and I entered, was a long counter. Several people stood in a line beneath a wooden sign hanging from the ceiling with "TO-GO" printed in bold white letters. Beyond that was a man and woman busy preparing orders.

Their movements shared a steady rhythm as if they'd been working as a team for a long time. The woman's dark red hair was pulled into a ponytail, the long curls swaying with her hurried activities. The man was older, and I guessed his age to be somewhere in his late fifties or early sixties.

"Morning, Owen," the man said to the next customer in line. "How are you doing?"

"Fine, fine," Owen replied, his tone brusque. "I'll have

16

a regular coffee, black, and make it to go." He nervously pulled out his wallet and glanced around.

"It's been a while since you've been in," the man said, fitting a lid on a Styrofoam cup. "Are they keeping you busy at the Promenade?"

"Yeah…I suppose," Owen said, then tossed some money on the counter. He gave our group a curt nod as he hastened for the door.

"That was Avery's boss," Delia said after the door shut behind Owen.

"Not a very nice man," Myrna said. "I'll never understand why they hired him to take over as manager instead of giving the job to my nephew Benjamin."

"Ben's the assistant manager," Vincent said to clarify.

"Come on. I want to introduce you to some more of my friends." Delia took my hand and pulled me toward an empty spot at the counter. Myrna and Vincent stopped a few feet behind us.

"Archer, Zoey," Delia said, drawing the man and woman's attention.

"Morning," they paused what they were doing and said in unison.

"This has to be Brinley, right?" Archer grinned as he wiped his hand on his brown apron, then stuck his arm over the counter. "Nice to meet you."

"You too," I said, shaking his hand. His demeanor was friendly and seemed genuine, not a practiced and professional persona that I occasionally encountered at food service places in the city.

"Archer's the owner of the Bean," Delia said. "And Zoey is the best pastry chef and espresso maker in town."

"Oh, I don't know about that, but thanks." Zoey's blush made the freckles running along the bridge of her nose and across her cheeks more prominent. "Why don't you go ahead and take a seat. I'll be with you as soon as I finish this order."

"What do you say we sit outside today?" Delia asked

the group, then motioned toward a glass door on the right side of two ceiling-to-floor window panes that offered a panoramic glimpse of the sandy beach and ocean. To the left were several palm trees, close enough to add ambiance to the landscape but not block anyone's view.

The heat and humidity hadn't reached a high level yet, so the weather was still pleasant, making it a great place to enjoy breakfast. I took a seat close to the railing, which allowed me to see a good portion of the beach. It also gave me the opportunity to watch the people strolling on the sidewalk and those who decided to stop at the coffee bar.

As far as locations went, Archer had picked an excellent spot for his business. Not only was it easily accessible to the locals, but it probably gained quite a few sales from the tourists who visited the nearby shops and the beach.

It wasn't long before Zoey showed up with only one menu and handed it to me. Delia and her friends either had the contents memorized or usually ordered the same thing. "I'll give you a few minutes to look things over," Zoey said, then headed back inside.

"Any recommendations?" I asked as I opened the laminated menu.

"It's all good," Delia said.

I searched for the drinks first, then perused what Archer had to offer. My aunt hadn't been kidding when she said there was a wide selection. He had everything from lattes to cappuccinos to macchiatos, along with an assortment of flavored coffees. I decided to stick with a regular brew but chose the caramel mocha blend.

Myrna had taken a seat on my right. "The scones are my favorites, but they have other things," she said, leaning closer and pointing at the list of breakfast items, which had a note stating that all items were freshly baked. The picture of an apple cinnamon muffin, with icing drizzled across the top and sides, had my mouthwatering and made my selection simple.

"Since you're going to be here for a week, you need to make sure Delia takes you sightseeing," Myrna said. "Oh, and you need to go down to the docks, and…"

Zoey appeared, putting an end to Myrna's rambling. "Everyone ready?" She held up a small pen and pad, then jotted down our orders.

Not long after that, Archer stepped outside, carrying a tray with our breakfast. "How do you like our quaint little town so far?" he asked after setting a tall mug filled with steaming coffee in front of me.

Enticed by the rich aroma, I inhaled a deep breath before answering. "I didn't get here until late last night. I haven't seen much, but the walk over was relaxing, and I enjoyed the scenery." I took a sip and groaned. "This is really good. I can see why Delia wanted to bring me here first."

"Wait until you try this," Archer chuckled, presenting a plate with a muffin that looked better than its picture.

"I can't wait," I said, picking up my fork, then savoring a bite.

The influx of customers entering the building had slowed since our arrival. I wasn't surprised when Archer leaned his back against the railing instead of returning inside.

"Do you have big plans for the day?" he asked.

"Nothing tentative," I said, glancing at Delia. "At least not yet."

"I thought I'd show her the shops, then see where we ended up," Delia said.

"Sounds like a plan," Archer said.

"I noticed you have a new sign on the front door," Delia said after swallowing a bite of her croissant. "When did you decide to hire a manager?"

Archer grinned. "You know how I've always wanted to take my boat out and spend more time fishing?"

"Uh-huh," Myrna said, picking up her latte and blowing on it.

"If I recall, you tell us about it at least once a week," Vincent said, pushing his empty plate aside.

Archer ignored Vincent's sarcasm. "Well, Zoey suggested I find somebody to run the place, so I don't have to be here all the time."

"Why don't you just have Zoey do it and hire someone to help her?" Delia asked.

"I already asked her, but all she wants to do is serve customers and do the baking," Archer said. "She has no interest in being in charge."

"Didn't you say Brinley has a lot of management experience?" Myrna asked, smiling at Delia.

"I may have mentioned it," Delia said, then gave her hand a nonchalant flick.

"Maybe you could give Archer some hiring pointers," Myrna said.

She couldn't have known about my upcoming relocation or how bad it made me feel. I tamped down the unwanted dread and forced a smile. I'd sat in on a couple of interviews, but any hiring done for our department went through human resources first. "I don't know anything about the food service industry, so I don't think I'd be very helpful."

"It's too bad you don't live here." The smile Myrna directed at me seemed rehearsed. If Delia hadn't already invited me to stay with her, the statement wouldn't have triggered my suspicious nature and made me wonder if my aunt and her friend were up to something.

It wouldn't be the first time that Delia had used subtle methods to get me to think about my future. Now that I thought about it, the topic of me living closer to her had come up in several of our conversations after she'd moved.

"Isn't it, though," I mumbled before draining the last of my drink.

"I need to go check on Zoey," Archer said, disappearing back inside. I couldn't tell if he really needed to get back to work or if he was saving me from having to answer any more questions. Either way, I was grateful.

"So, Delia, have you decided where you two are going first?" Vincent asked.

"I thought we'd start with a tour of the main street, then maybe do some shopping," Delia said.

"Be careful, Brinley. The way these two like to shop,"—Vincent's gaze jumped from Myrna to Delia—"you'll be busy most of the day."

Myrna scowled at Vincent. "I'm pretty sure that's the point." She continued by listing the names of different shops and which ones she insisted we needed to visit. I tuned out the conversation when I heard whining that sounded like it was coming from underneath the patio deck.

Curious to find out if an animal was in distress, I leaned closer to the railing, trying to get a glimpse of whatever was making the noise. When that didn't work, I pushed out of my chair. I walked to the end of the patio, which, unfortunately, stopped at the end of the building.

"Brinley, what are you doing?" Delia asked.

"I thought I heard something," I said, straining to listen and wishing I could see through the leaves of the tall shrubs running along the side of the deck.

"I didn't hear anything," Delia said.

Vincent didn't say anything but seemed intrigued and straightened in his chair.

"What did it sound like?" Myrna asked.

A whimper followed by a bark answered her question for me. I turned around and headed for the stairs. Delia was the first one to get to her feet and trail after me.

"It sounded like it was coming from over here." When I walked around the corner of the deck, I spotted the back end of a small dog. I took a few steps closer and was relieved to see that the animal wasn't hurt. Most of its fur was reddish-brown. A patch of white covered the muzzle, the chest, and the front of its legs. Its long, straggly coat also looked as if it hadn't been washed in a long time. I had a soft spot for dogs and cats and was determined to find out what was upsetting the poor little thing.

It seemed that whatever was agitating him had found its way under the deck. Dirt and small plants flew through the air as he frantically pawed at one of the painted wooden panels that ran along the structure's base. I didn't think Archer would be happy when he saw the destruction the dog had caused to his nicely manicured landscaping.

"What do you think he's after?" Delia asked.

"I don't know, but I think we should find out," I said, hoping that my curiosity didn't end with me getting bit. "Hey there, boy," I cooed as I inched toward the busy animal. From this angle, I couldn't tell if the dog was a male or a female. To me, his cute little face said boy, so I went with it.

The dog jerked his head in my direction as if noticing me for the first time. Instead of growling like I'd expected, he walked over to me and sniffed my ankle. Satisfied that I wasn't a threat, he rose up on his hind legs and pawed my bare leg, leaving a trail of mud on my skin. After contently allowing me to scratch behind his ears, he dropped to the ground and returned to making more of a mess.

Animals communicated in their own way, and if you paid close attention, it wasn't difficult to figure out what they wanted. When he looked up at me and made another doggy noise, I assumed he wanted my help. "Okay, let's see what you found," I said as I stepped over the discarded plants to get a better look at what was bothering him.

Painted wooden panels had been attached to the bottom edge of the building's frame, no doubt to keep anything from crawling underneath. It looked as if a couple of the screws had been removed. Several panels appeared to be loose, but one was in worse shape than the others. It was hanging at an angle, forming a narrow gap between the one next to it.

"Brinley, please be careful," Delia said. "You never know what might be in there."

Thanks to my aunt's comment, my mind was filled with images of a smaller, fiercer animal. One with pointy teeth and sharp claws. The idea of a creature pouncing on me had me hesitating to pull back the decorative sheet of wood.

"It would definitely be a good place to hide a dead body," Vincent said, his voice speculative.

"You could be right," Myrna said.

A body would be worse, and I groaned. Not because it wasn't possible, but because it was. I'd seen plenty of crime shows and read enough articles to know that the police found corpses in lots of dark, out-of-the-way places. What worried me more was that Myrna and Vincent had thought about it in the first place.

After shooting a sarcastic thanks-for-sharing glare at the three observers who were now standing behind me eagerly waiting to see what I'd find, I reached for the panel again. It didn't take much effort to make the gap wider, and what I found inside the hole hissed and flashed its teeth. When a tabby cat sprang through the opening and raced past me, I shrieked and fell backward, my backside landing in the dirt.

The dog did what dogs do best; it started barking and gave chase. Obviously, the intent was not to catch and kill but to let the cat know it had infringed on his territory. Once the cat skirted around a palm tree and disappeared, the dog gave a final yip and returned to our group.

"Well, that was disappointing," Vincent said, after holding out his hand and helping me off the ground.

"Maybe not," Myrna said, drawing everyone's attention to the duffel bag sitting near the opening I'd made when I moved the panel. A dark blue bag I hadn't noticed since I was too busy avoiding a cat attack.

I finished dusting off the back of my shorts, then, after giving the area behind the bag a wary glance, I grabbed the bag, stepped away from the landscaped area, and set it on the ground.

The bag was about two feet long, had a closed zipper running between the fabric handles along the top, and bulged in all directions. It hadn't been overly heavy to move, but it hadn't been light either.

The four of us, or I should say five if I counted Harley, who was sitting next to my right leg, had formed a circle around the bag.

"Maybe it's only part of a body," Vincent said, raising one end of his lips. "Like a severed head or something."

"Vincent," Delia said, smacking his arm. "What a morbid thought."

Vincent grunted, and for the first time since I'd met him, he came close to smiling.

Myrna bent forward to squint at the bag through her bifocals. "I say we open it and see what's inside."

CHAPTER FOUR

It turned out that when Myrna suggested *we* open the bag, she'd really meant me. A consensus that everyone else in the group had agreed with. Logically, I believed the odds of finding body parts were low, yet I couldn't completely dispel the thought of opening the bag and discovering the eyes from a severed head staring at me.

I couldn't even count on the dog to support having someone else perform the task. After sniffing the bag, he'd pawed it a couple of times before taking a seat on the ground next to me, then stared up at me with expectant dark brown eyes. "Don't you have a cat to chase or something else you should be doing?"

The dog barked and swished his short curled tail, letting me know he was exactly where he thought he should be. I couldn't believe a few scratches behind the ears and assisting with a bit of feline recon had earned me a new friend so quickly.

As curious as everyone was to see what was inside the bag, myself included, I considered where I'd found it and worried that we might be infringing on Archer's personal and private property. Though I couldn't come up with a reasonable explanation for him to stash a bag under his deck, I still believed in doing some due diligence. "Maybe we should check with Archer first," I said.

"Check with me about what?" Archer asked as he rounded the corner of the building.

Getting caught after mentioning his name brought heat to my cheeks and made me jump. "Check with you about this," I said, taking a step back so he could wedge between Delia and me.

Archer raised an inquiring brow. "What have you got there, and why would you need to ask me about it?"

"Because we found it underneath the building," Delia said, tipping her head toward the gap in the panels. "Is it yours?"

"No," Archer said, sounding perplexed. "Why were you looking under the building?" He narrowed his eyes, taking in the destruction. "And what happened to my plants?"

"The dog was trying to get at a cat that had slipped underneath the deck," Delia said.

"I'm afraid he got a little rambunctious in his efforts," I said, hoping to pacify Archer's anger. There was something endearing about the dog, and I couldn't resist leaning over to protectively scratch his head.

"How did you get Harley to mind you like that?" Archer said, seemingly more impressed with the dog's behavior than the damage he'd caused. "He's never done anything like that for me."

I was baffled by the cute little animal myself. "Other than giving him some attention, nothing. He sat down and stayed all by himself." It usually took some time for animals to warm up to strangers and quite a bit of training for them to follow commands. Apparently, I wasn't the only one surprised to see that the dog hadn't left my side.

"When did you get a dog?" Myrna asked Archer.

"Oh, he's not mine," Archer said. "Or Zoey's either."

I glanced down at the scruffy dog who was practically sitting on my foot and noted the way he perked his ears as if he knew we were talking about him. "Does he belong to someone else in the neighborhood?" I asked.

The people who lived next door to my family growing up had a Bulldog who was experienced in the art of escaping from his fenced-in yard. I hated to think there might be a child somewhere, upset and crying that their pet had gone missing?

"I'm pretty sure he's a stray," Archer said. "He's been hanging around the area for the last couple of months but doesn't usually show up until late afternoon. I think someone may have abandoned him."

"If he's a stray, then how do you know his name is Harley?" I asked, staring down at the dog. Harley was an unusual name, but it seemed to fit the scraggly animal perfectly.

Archer shrugged. "I don't. That's what Zoey started calling him, and the name stuck. She's been handing out names to all kinds of critters ever since I can remember. Even the fish in the tank inside all have names."

"I'll bet he'll come to just about anything if there's food involved," Archer said, scratching his chin. "Though I've never seen him take to anyone before. He usually comes close enough for handouts, then disappears."

"Now that we've established the dog's history and that he seems to like Brinley, do you think we can get back to finding out what's inside the bag?" Vincent grumbled.

"People occasionally forget stuff on the beach, but no one's ever messed with the panels or left anything under there before," Archer said. "So yeah, I'd definitely like to know what's inside." He crouched next to the bag and tugged on the zipper, which was fine by me since I still had images of body parts floating around in my mind.

As soon as Archer had the bag open and was peeling back the sides, everyone, including me, bent forward to view the contents. Archer reached inside and pulled out a silver candlestick.

"That's not at all what I expected," Vincent said, not

bothering to hide his disappointment.

"Me neither," Myrna said, straightening.

As soon as Archer pulled out the expensive-looking jewelry box, I wondered if the items had been stolen. "I don't know about you guys, but this stuff looks like it might have come from a robbery."

"Do you think this stuff belongs to Bridget Driscoll?" Myrna asked. "I heard her house was broken into a couple of months ago."

Somehow, I didn't think the bag had been sitting under the deck for that long. It was too bad there was no way to prove my theory. Between the dog, cat, and me, any evidence of fresh footprints, if there'd been any, had been destroyed. "I think maybe we should call the police and let them deal with it," I said.

Delia tapped Archer's shoulder. "I'm not sure how our local law enforcement handles robberies, but you might not want to touch anything else in case they decide to dust for fingerprints."

"You might be right," Archer said, returning the items he was holding, then pulling a cell phone out of his back pocket as he pushed to his feet.

Once Archer had finished his call, he said, "The police will have questions and would like everyone to wait here." After zipping the bag, he picked it up.

"Shouldn't we leave the bag here?" Myrna asked.

"We've already tampered with the evidence, so leaving it where you found it seems moot," Archer said. "Besides, taking it with us will keep someone else from making off with it." He motioned toward the front of the building. "Come on, and I'll get you another round of drinks on the house."

Though it sounded like he was talking about something stronger, I knew he meant coffee, which at this point, sounded like a great idea. "Let's go, Harley," I said to see if the dog would follow us. Up until that moment, I thought his attentiveness was a fluke and was shocked when he barked and followed after me.

I was glad the patio was empty of customers when we returned to our table. It would make things easier when the police arrived. Archer had been thinking the same thing because he muttered something about keeping the nosy locals inside before he set the bag next to the railing and went to prepare our drinks.

About five minutes later, Zoey arrived carrying a tray. "Wow, I thought Archer was joking when he said you got Harley to mind," she said as she stepped around him and set a drink down in front of me.

For whatever reason, the dog decided to stay with our group and found a spot near my chair to lay down on his belly.

"He never sticks around." Zoey circled the table, delivering the rest of the drinks. "He's usually a grab-a-snack-and-go kind of dog." She tucked the empty tray under her arm and stared at me as if I'd worked a miracle on the animal.

"Other than scratch his head and help him scare a poor cat, I didn't really do much," I said. "Although, if I'd known it was a cat he was after, I probably wouldn't have moved the panel." I still felt bad about making the cat a target, even if Harley hadn't intended to hurt it.

"Yes, but if you hadn't moved the panel, then you wouldn't have found the bag," Delia said, picking up her mug.

"And if the stuff inside was stolen, then you did a good deed and made the owners happy," Myrna added.

"We don't know for sure that the items were stolen," Vincent said.

It was a theory I hoped the police would validate one way or another once they arrived.

"You're just upset that your severed head idea didn't pan out," Myrna teased, earning her a scowl.

If we'd been in the city, it would've taken at least a half-hour, maybe longer, for local law enforcement to show up, but in this much smaller community, it had taken less time for someone to arrive—on foot. There were no visible roads nearby, so I assumed there must be a public parking lot in the general vicinity. Hence, the reason the man wearing a green deputy's uniform approached the Flavored Bean using the sidewalk that ran along the front of the building. He walked with a confident stride, his gaze alert to his surroundings.

Archer must've been watching from the window inside. Once the police official got closer, he stepped outside and said something about being right back, then headed down the stairs to greet him.

Delia clapped her hands together. "I was hoping they'd send Carson."

"Why? Do you know him?" I asked. My aunt had always been a social person and knew a lot of people, but I was surprised her circle of acquaintances included someone in law enforcement.

"Of course. He occasionally attends events at the Promenade." Delia grinned. "He's a really good dancer and quite handsome, don't you think?"

"And single," Myrna added, wiggling her brows.

Any woman in the area would have a hard time not noticing Carson's broad shoulders or the way his uniform clung nicely to his tall, muscular frame. "Yes, he's nice-looking," I said, trying to keep my voice neutral. I had a feeling if my aunt and her friend detected the slightest hint of interest, I'd be spending the rest of my vacation avoiding their matchmaking efforts.

The last thing I needed was a new boyfriend, especially since dating Rick had led to a relocation promotion. A problem I still had no idea how I was going to handle. Even so, I couldn't help giving Carson an admiring glance while he spent the next few minutes talking to Archer and jotting down notes in a small pad he'd retrieved from his shirt pocket. They'd kept their voices low, so I couldn't hear their conversation. Archer appeared uncomfortable and glanced in our direction several times before responding to whatever Carson had asked him.

"Can you hear what they're saying?" Myrna asked Vincent since he was sitting the closest.

"No," Vincent groaned and tapped his right ear. "My hearing isn't what it used to be."

"Your hearing's fine," Delia said. "I can't hear them either." It wasn't from a lack of trying. If my aunt leaned any farther out of her chair, she was going to tip over.

Archer pointed to the end of the building, then led Carson around the corner, no doubt showing him where we'd found the bag. A few minutes later, they reappeared and joined us on the deck. "This this it?" Carson asked Archer as he walked over to the bag.

"Yeah," Archer said. "If you don't need me for anything else, I need to get back inside and help Zoey." He hitched his thumb at the door.

"Not a problem, but please don't leave. I may have more questions." Carson pushed his sunglasses on top of his head, then knelt down to inspect the bag. He didn't touch anything inside, but judging by the look on his face, I got the impression he recognized some of the contents.

Once he was finished, he got to his feet and directed his attention to our table.

"Everyone," Carson said, acknowledging all of us with the tip of his head.

"Good morning, Carson," Myrna said, fluffing her short silver curls. "Or should we address you as Deputy Pritchett since you're on duty?"

I thought it odd that a deputy and not an officer had shown up to deal with a possible theft. The town wasn't overly large, so maybe its police department had a small staff.

"Carson's fine," he said, his dark gaze moving to me. "And you are?"

"This is my niece, Brinley," Delia said. "She's staying with me for a week, maybe longer."

My aunt and I hadn't talked about extending my visit. I couldn't have stayed even if I wanted to, not with a relocation deadline scheduled a few weeks after I returned home. The last part of her statement might have been an innocent slip, but knowing my aunt, I didn't think so. If she was up to something, asking her to clarify in front of the deputy during his investigation wouldn't be appropriate.

"It's nice to meet you, and welcome to Hawkins Harbor," Carson said. "I hope you enjoy your stay." He held up the notepad and pen he'd used earlier when he spoke to Archer. "If you don't mind, I have a few questions."

"Not at all," I said.

"I understand it was your dog that found the goods," Carson said.

Harley hadn't left, but he'd warily eyed Carson before moving under my chair and sitting on his haunches. When the dog whined, I gave his head a reassuring pat. "He's not..." Delia gave my arm a squeeze to keep me from finishing.

"I noticed that you don't have a leash," Carson said. "You might want to use one while you're here." Though his tone was polite, there was no missing the underlying directive.

"We'll take care of it right away," Delia said.

My aunt knew that I didn't need the additional complication of caring for a pet. I had no idea why she didn't want me to correct Carson's assumption about the dog's ownership and decided to wait until later to ask her.

After giving Delia a curt nod, Carson returned his gaze to me. "Why don't you tell me how you found the bag?"

He'd already talked to Archer, so I wasn't sure why he needed to hear my version of what happened. Were my aunt and her friends right about the bag's contents being stolen? Was it possible that Archer had made the top of Carson's suspect list? The bag had been found hidden on

Archer's property, so it was a reasonable assumption.

I spent the next several minutes giving him a detailed account of everything that had transpired, leaving out how the cat had scared me, and I'd ended up on my backside. I was sure the ungraceful event wasn't pertinent to his investigation.

"Did any of you see anything or know how the bag got underneath the deck?" Carson asked. I suspected it was the same question he'd already asked Archer.

"What about Archer?" Carson looked up from the pad. "Did it seem like he knew why the bag was there?"

"No," I said before anyone else could answer. Even though I'd only met Archer, he'd seemed genuinely surprised when I found the bag. I was a relatively good judge of character and would be shocked if I discovered he'd been involved.

Delia pushed to her feet and slapped her hands on her hips. "You don't think Archer had something to do with this, do you?"

"Delia." Carson softened his tone, trying to placate her. "Archer owns the building, and it's a question I had to ask."

Archer picked that moment to step outside. He placed his hand on my aunt's shoulder. "It's okay, Delia. Carson's just doing his job."

"Well, we don't have to like," Myrna said, getting out of her chair to stand on Delia's other side.

"I'll be in touch if I have any more questions." Carson slipped his pen and pad back in his pocket, then picked up the bag. "In the meantime, if any of you think of anything else, please don't hesitate to call." He made it as far as the bottom step before stopping.

"Oh, and I expect you three,"—Carson locked eyes with Myrna, Vincent, and my aunt—"not to do any freelancing."

Freelancing? I raised a questioning brow at Delia, who responded with a shrug. Myrna batted her eyelashes innocently, and Vincent opened his mouth as if he was going to say something, then tightly clamped his lips together.

Satisfied that no one was going to argue with him, Carson finished his descent and headed along the sidewalk in the same direction he'd arrived. I waited until he was out of hearing distance, then turned to Delia and asked, "Why didn't you want him to know that Harley isn't my dog?"

"Carson likes to follow the rules, and Harley is a stray," Delia said. "I was afraid if you told him the truth, he'd turn the dog over to animal control."

"Did you consider what would happen when Carson comes back and sees Harley running loose?" I asked, not bothering to hide my irritation. The last thing I needed was the handsome deputy showing up at my aunt's house to find out why my supposed pet was roaming the neighborhood, especially after he'd warned me about using a leash.

Hearing my distressed voice must have upset Harley. He whined and rubbed his head against my leg. "It's okay, boy," I said, reaching down to give him a reassuring scratch.

"Carson's not going to find Harley running around loose," Delia said, smirking with satisfaction.

"And why is that?" I asked, eying her warily.

"Because you're going to adopt him and bring him home with us." She quickly held up her hand to keep me from arguing. "Temporarily, I mean... Until we can find him a good home."

It was hard to dispute her kind heart, even if she'd volunteered me for the role of a new pet owner. "What about Luna?" I asked, knowing her cat's reaction wasn't going to be pretty. "Did you also consider how she is going to react when you bring a dog into her home?"

Delia sighed. "I know it will be an adjustment, but I'm sure Luna will be fine."

"Great," Vincent said. "Now that we have that settled, what are we going to do to keep Archer from being blamed for the robberies?"

Archer had gone back inside right after Carson left; otherwise, I had a feeling he would try to dissuade his friends from getting involved. "Don't you think you should let the police handle this?" I asked.

"I'm sure Carson is quite capable of doing a good job, but from what I've heard, the police still have no idea who the culprit was in Bridget's case," Myrna said.

"Heard from who?" I asked.

"We have an information network over at the Promenade," Myrna said.

"Oh," I said. Having been raised in a small town, I knew that her network was the elderly woman's equivalent of a gossip chain.

"If something happens to Archer and he has to shut down the Bean, then where will we go for breakfast?" Myrna asked.

"We're not going to let anything happen to Archer or the Bean." Vincent reached across the table and gave Myrna's hand a pat.

"I agree," Delia said. "I think we should get together later and discuss a plan of action. Say around six at my place."

"A plan of action... What?" I didn't get a chance to finish my question. Everyone was already pushing away from the table when Zoey arrived, carrying a collar and leash.

"Here, you can use these to get Harley home," she said, handing them to me. "I was hoping to snag him before the catcher got a hold of him, but he's been very evasive. I'm actually jealous that you got him to come to you and stay. How did you do it?"

"I'm still trying to figure that one out," I said, squatting down and slipping the collar around his neck. Harley squirmed a little but didn't try to bolt. If Zoey had gone to the trouble of getting a leash, then maybe she'd planned to make the dog her pet.

I was already getting attached to the little guy and felt a twinge of remorse about turning him over to someone else's care. I reminded myself that I was the visitor in this scenario and didn't want to interfere with Zoey's plans. After snapping the leash to the collar's clip, I stood and held the looped end out to her.

"Oh, no, no, no," Zoey said, waving me off. "Harley's made his choice, and I highly approve."

CHAPTER FIVE

Shortly after Delia, Myrna, and Vincent decided to help Archer and meet at my aunt's place later, customers filtered outside to occupy several tables. Now that Carson was gone, there was no reason for Archer to keep people from coming out onto the deck. Not long after that, our group decided it was time to leave.

When I'd first heard Delia's plan to have me adopt Harley, I'd been reluctant. But the more I thought about him ending up in a cage at the animal control facility, the more determined I became to find him a good home. Getting him cleaned up and settled at Delia's house had taken the place of leisurely shopping, at least for today.

Unique shops were a trademark for small towns. When Delia suggested stopping by Pemshaw's Pet Boutique before heading back to her place, I imagined a place similar to a hair salon for people. I'd gotten the hair care part right. One-half of the shop was designed to accommodate all types of grooming needs, including baths, hair, and nail clipping.

The other half contained shelves stocked with a wide variety of pet care products. One entire wall was dedicated to fish and filled with rows of active aquariums, the dwellers both tropical and saltwater.

Pets were obviously welcome because I wasn't the only one walking around with a dog. Once again, I was thankful Zoey had loaned me a collar and leash.

We'd barely taken a few steps when my aunt's name echoed through the room. A woman walked toward us with a boisterous bounce in her step. Her curvy figure filled out a uniform comprised of black pants and a short-sleeved pink top that zipped along the front and had two large pockets positioned below her waist. The color of her hair, a shade of blonde created by a professional stylist, was held away from her face with a pair of combs.

"This is Leona Pemshaw," Delia said. "She owns this fine establishment and has the best pet grooming services in town."

Leona's flushed cheeks were brighter than her top. "Who's this?" she asked as she bent down over to let Harley sniff her hand. After he gave her palm an approving lick, she reached up to run her fingers through the hair on his head.

"Brinley's new dog," Delia answered with a grin. She'd made it sound as if I'd gone to the trouble of hand-selecting the dog myself rather than being coerced into the temporary role of pet owner.

"Brinley, as in your niece?" Leona stood and held out her hand. "Delia's told me all about you. It's nice to finally meet you."

"You as well," I said, shooting a sidelong glance at my aunt, wondering just how much she'd shared with Leona and possibly anyone else she knew. Delia was quite the socializer, and it appeared that I was one of her favorite topics.

Leona tucked her hands into the pockets of her smock. "I heard Carson got called over to the Bean this morning and left carrying a duffel bag," she said. "Any idea what that was all about?"

I assumed the coffee bar's ideal location made it

convenient for store owners to grab their drinks and breakfast to-go before heading to work. No doubt quite a few customers had come and gone when we were talking to the deputy. The news probably reached every business along the street long before Delia and I had arrived with Harley.

If Leona knew that Carson had been at the Bean, then she also knew that we were the ones he'd been there to see. I had to give her credit for the nonchalant, rather than nosy, way of trying to find out what happened.

Being new in town and unsure how things worked, I didn't want to be responsible for more information hitting the so-called network than was necessary. Instead of responding to Leona's question, I decided to let Delia take the lead.

"Harley had cornered a cat behind the panels running along the deck, and when we went to see what the commotion was all about, Brinley found the bag."

Leona rolled her eyes. "That seems like an odd place to find a bag. Did Carson have any idea how long it had been there or who might have put it there in the first place?"

"You know Carson and his strict rules," Delia said.

"Right," Leona said. "No discussing details about work." She flashed a conspiratorial grin. "Please tell me you looked inside."

"We might have taken a quick peek before Brinley suggested we report it to the police," Delia said.

"Well, what did you see?" Leona asked excitedly.

Delia glanced around to make sure no other customers could hear her. "All I saw was a silver candlestick and a small heart-shaped jewelry box. Both of them looked expensive."

Leona's eyes widened, then, after doing an interior scan of her own, she said, "That sounds like Ellie Poverly's stuff. She was in here yesterday and said her place had been robbed over the weekend."

"Really, I hadn't heard," Delia said, her voice laced with

concern. "Ellie only lives a few blocks from my place."

I was beginning to think that gleaning tidbits of information was one of the reasons we'd stopped here instead of going to a grocery store that most likely carried everything we'd need for Harley.

"What about Archer?" Leona asked, clearly not ready to give up her quest for information. "Did he have any ideas?"

Though it didn't sound like Leona thought Archer was responsible for the theft, I was glad Delia had omitted Carson's speculation about his involvement. I didn't envy the deputy his job and knew it would go a lot smoother if everyone in town didn't make him out to be the bad guy.

"No, he was as surprised as we were." Delia shrugged. "That's all we know at the moment."

"I see," Leona said, smiling at me with renewed interest. "Did you tell Brinley that Carson was single?"

"No, Myrna beat me to it." Delia's dejected tone made it sound as if she were competing with her friend.

"Did she like him?" Leona asked.

Delia glanced at me. "Not that she's mentioned."

Words escaped me, and I gaped at the two women. I couldn't believe they were discussing my dating prospects as if I weren't standing here.

"That's okay. If she doesn't like Carson, then maybe you should think about having her take Harley to see the vet. Ever since Jackson moved to town, pet sales have been wonderful," Leona said. "I don't think there's a single female in the area who wouldn't like to gain his attention."

My lack of a decent love life wasn't even on my list of concerns at the moment. Neither was having others play matchmaker for me. "You two realize I'm only going to be here for a week, right?" I asked.

"That doesn't mean you have to spend every minute with me or that you can't have a little fun while you're here," Delia said.

"Trying to get rid of me already?" I asked.

"You know better than that." Delia frowned and pulled me into a hug, which made me feel bad for teasing her.

"Taking Harley in for a checkup and shots is actually a good idea," I said, shifting the conversation in a safer direction. The dog, who'd been patiently sitting at my feet, wasn't in the best condition, so who knew what kind of care he'd had before he ended up living on the streets. "I'll go only if you promise not to try hooking me up with the vet."

My concession seemed to satisfy both women and put an end to any further information sharing. Leona clasped her hands together. "Did you need something for Luna, or was there something else I can help you with today?" She gave Harley an eager glance. "Maybe a bath and grooming treatment."

Apparently, Harley understood the word "Bath" and wanted no part of it. He whined, scooted behind my legs, and shuddered. The dog was filthy, smelled, and in desperate need of a cleaning. We were still getting to know each other, and I didn't have the heart to force the ministrations of a stranger on him. "For the time being, I think I'll handle giving him a...you know." I spelled out the word that had upset him.

"I understand," Leona chuckled. "Do you need supplies?"

"Do we?" I asked Delia since bringing the dog home had been her idea. She hadn't mentioned whether or not rescuing dogs was a regular occurrence, so I had no idea if she kept the necessary items on hand in her home.

"We do," she said.

"Then follow me." Leona took the lead and directed us to an aisle where the shelves on one side were filled with dog care items. I felt a tug on the leash and found Harley sniffing bags of dog food, his curled tail wagging rapidly.

"I think we're going to need a cart," I said after realizing I'd need more than a bottle of shampoo and a collar and leash to replace the ones Zoey had loaned me.

"Let me grab you one." Leona headed toward the front of the shop and returned a minute later, pushing a miniature version of the kind used in grocery stores. The cart's frame was metal, but the basket was white plastic with black paw prints randomly scattered along the outside surface. "If you need anything else, please let me know."

As soon as Leona walked away to help another customer, Delia leaned closer and whispered, "The information you get here is way better than what you'll hear over at the hair salon."

It sounded to me like the information network Myrna relied on extended past the confines of the Promenade. I wouldn't be surprised if my aunt and her friends had contacts all over Hawkins Harbor.

Harley yipped and pawed my leg, reminding me to focus on shopping. Though Delia and I had stopped at a designated potty area on our way here to let the dog take care of business, I worried that he might have an accident before we got back outside.

Shampoo was the first item to go into the cart, followed by a dark blue leash with a matching collar. Harley had lived on the streets and struggled to find his next meal, so I didn't think he'd be a finicky eater, not like Luna. Even so, I chose the bag on the shelf he'd gone from sniffing to pawing.

When we reached the toy section, I snagged a yellow ball and a hedgehog that squeaked when I squeezed it. "Which one?" I asked, holding them both out for the dog's perusal.

Harley sat back on his haunches and barked.

"Both it is." I chuckled, then tossed the toys in the cart.

"Is there anything else you need," Delia asked when we'd reached the other end of the aisle.

I stared at the contents in the cart and knew I'd probably gone a little overboard, especially for an animal who wouldn't be in my life for very long. I didn't care. This was my vacation, and doing something good and selfless felt wonderful.

I'd always wanted a dog, but my mother refused to allow any kind of animal in the house. Even a bowl with a single gold fish had been off-limits. After I'd moved out on my own, I'd promised myself that I would eventually get a furry companion. Something that never happened.

There'd been times when I could barely afford to feed myself, let alone an animal, so getting a pet had been put on hold, along with a lot of other things I was starting to regret.

"I think we're good," I said, knowing that my aunt would be more than happy to come back if I'd forgotten anything. I turned the cart around, being careful not to run over Harley in the process, and headed toward the checkout counter near the front of the shop. "Come on, little guy. It's time to show you your new home."

CHAPTER SIX

The cart full of supplies I'd purchased at Leona's place had ended up filling three large plastic bags. The cute doggy bed with bones printed on the fabric took up a bag by itself. Without a car, Delia and I had to carry them back to her place.

For the most part, Harley hadn't been difficult to lead. Either he'd had some previous leash training, or he was content to pace along beside me. The only time he gave me trouble was when we encountered other people. It was like we'd hit rush hour traffic for owners out walking their dogs. Thankfully, it happened less frequently once we moved away from the shops and reached the sidewalk near the beach.

In order to carry the bags, I'd looped the end of Harley's leash around my wrist. By the time we'd reached Delia's house, my arm was tired from the dog's excessive tugging so he could bark, happily prance around strangers, or stop and sniff their animals. The barking encouraged hasty retreats, and the sniffing encouraged cooing and head scratches.

"Do you think it's okay to let Harley off his leash?" I asked Delia once we were inside the house and I'd placed the bag's containing his new belongings on the kitchen table. I worried how Luna would react to having a dog running around in her domain and scanned the area searching for her. When I didn't see any sign of the cat, I assumed she must be napping somewhere upstairs and was too lazy to make an appearance.

"I'm sure it will be fine," Delia said, placing her bags next to mine.

Worrying about altercations between Luna and Harley would've been less stressful if I could let him run around outside. Delia's front yard wasn't fenced, and her backyard consisted of a deck that faced the ocean.

After unclipping the leash, I nervously watched Harley as he wandered around the living room, smelling furniture and anything else that crossed his path. "Aren't you afraid he'll have an accident?" I asked Delia.

"Don't worry. Most of the floors are tiled, so it will be easy to clean up any of his little indiscretions."

I knew I'd have to take Harley for walks and had included pet waste bags in my purchase in case there weren't any handy posts equipped with disposal units close to my aunt's house. Cleaning up after the animal wasn't something I looked forward to, and I hoped to mitigate as many of his minor accidents as possible.

Delia remembered how Harley had reacted to Leona's mention of a decent grooming, and waited for him to reach the other side of the room before suggesting I give him a bath. "You can use the downstairs bathroom at the end of the hall," she said, then pointed. "There are extra towels in the storage closet." On her way to the kitchen, Delia glanced over her shoulder. "I'll distract him with a snack so you can get everything ready."

All the towels lining the shelves were high quality, in good condition, and not something I would use to bathe a dog. I searched until I found a couple that looked a little older, then placed them on the closed toilet, and ran a few inches of warm water in the bathtub.

After coaxing Harley into my arms, I took the shampoo bottle from Delia and headed for the bathroom. Getting the dog into the tub took a little effort but was less challenging than keeping him in the water so I could scrub him. By the time I was finished, Harley and I were both soaked from top to bottom.

I was sitting in the middle of the floor, attempting to dry off the dog, when Delia opened the door that I'd closed to minimize escape. She held up her cell phone, aimed the miniature camera lens in my direction, and said, "Smile."

Instead, I frowned because her distraction cost me. The towel slipped, giving Harley the opportunity to shake his body and spray me with water droplets. "Delia, what are you doing?" I asked, scowling and wrangling the dog with the towel again.

She grinned and snapped another picture. "Starting your photo album, of course."

Being childless, I'd forgotten that my aunt viewed pets as children and was notorious for snapping shots of whatever she considered momentous occasions. Luna had her own album on Delia's phone, and I had one on my computer since I saved every picture she'd ever sent me of her not-so-darling cat. I received at least one text a month, sometimes more, which included photos of Luna's cutest antics along with assorted emojis.

I didn't want to ruin my aunt's fun by reminding her that starting an album of Harley and me was pointless since he'd be going to a new home within the week.

A melodic chime sounded from her phone, announcing a text. Delia glanced at the screen, then smiled. "I hope you don't mind sandwiches for dinner. Myrna is stopping by the deli on her way here."

Technically, I was on vacation and supposed to be relaxing, so I didn't have a problem keeping things simple. After hearing my life was being uprooted, stress had been a constant companion. I lived alone, so cooking wasn't one of my better talents, not that I couldn't prepare a decent meal if required. "Sandwiches sound great," I said, snagging the last dry towel and going to work on Harley's fur again.

Naturally, Luna picked that moment to show up and rub against Delia's leg. The taunting was all it took for Harley to bark, squirm loose, and chase after the cat. Delia squeaked and grabbed the door frame as the dog raced past her.

"Still think this was a good idea?" I giggled, gripping the edge of the sink to pull myself off the floor.

Delia snorted. "I'm sure everything will be fine. They just need some time to get to know each other."

I heard a loud thud coming from the living room and said, "I hope you're right because I'm not sure your house is going to survive the adjustment period."

Delia shook her head, then hurried down the hallway. Having the two animals under the same roof had been her idea, so I didn't have a problem letting her deal with the two miscreants while I picked up the soggy towels and draped them along the rim of the bathtub. When I finally reached the living room, I found Harley sitting in the middle of the tiled floor staring up at Luna, who'd found an out-of-the-reach spot on a shelf lined with books.

The cat, pretending to be unaffected by the dog's presence, sat with her tail hanging over the edge and licking her front paw. I quickly scanned the room and didn't see anything out of place or broken. Delia had either returned whatever hit the floor to its original location, or its broken pieces were now residing in the trash.

"Harley," I said, shaking my finger at the dog. "If you don't behave yourself and quit tormenting Luna, you're going to spend the rest of the night locked in my room."

As if understanding what I'd said, the dog groaned, then walked over and head-butted my leg.

The doorbell rang, and Delia went to see who had arrived. "Heard a ruckus. Is everything okay in here?" I'd already discovered that Vincent wasn't much for pleasantries, something that Delia and Myrna didn't appear to mind.

"Everything's fine," Delia said.

"Good, then where do you want me to set up?" he asked, barely giving her time to move out of the way before walking inside.

"There should be room in my office," Delia said.

I was curious to know why my aunt hadn't asked Vincent about the tripod stand and large rectangular white board he carried down the hallway. They hadn't discussed any particulars about their get-together during our breakfast at the Bean, so I figured Delia must have contacted Vincent and Myrna while I was wrestling Harley in the bathtub.

"Delia, what's with the board?" I asked, watching Vincent disappear into one of the rooms.

"Vincent likes to be thorough when we investigate," Delia said. "Normally, we meet at his place, but since you're visiting and we have Harley to think about, I thought it would be better to set up here."

If I interpreted what my aunt had said correctly, it sounded like the three friends met regularly. It was wondering what they did, and why, that concerned me. "Exactly what do you investigate?" I asked.

"Murders." Delia walked over and draped her arm across my shoulders. "Sometimes other crimes, but mostly murders." Her tone said she was serious, and I didn't need a mirror to know that my face had paled. I sucked in a breath hoping to bring color back to my skin before she noticed.

The room across the hall from Delia's bedroom looked more like an entertainment area than an office. She did have a desk, along with a computer set up in a corner near the window. The other half of the room had a television screen mounted to the wall, which faced a cushioned sofa wide enough to comfortably seat three people. Adjacent and angled to form part of a square was a matching chair.

Vincent had set up his tripod and board in the corner not far from the screen. He'd even brought along some colored markers, which he'd placed on the stand at the base of the board.

A few minutes later, the doorbell chimed again, and Myrna swept into the room. The smell of food wafting through the air had gotten Harley's attention, and he eagerly trailed after her, his tail wagging rapidly as he'd followed her. After greetings and before another one of her breath-stealing hugs, she placed the take-out bags on the rectangular coffee table sitting in front of the sofa.

I selected a ham and cheese sandwich, a small bag of chips, and a bottled water from Delia's assortment of drinks. I'd barely settled into the chair and balanced a paper plate on my lap before Harley found a spot near my feet, his gaze never leaving my sandwich, even when I raised it to take a bite.

I might not have had any pets of my own growing up, but some of my childhood friends did. I learned enough from them to know that feeding dogs scraps wasn't healthy for the animal. Harley had already polished off the bowl of food I'd set out for him in the kitchen. I wondered how long it would take for me to crack under the pressure of his cute little doggy face and occasional pathetic whimper.

"Harley looks so much better," Myrna said. "Did you take him to Leona's place?"

"We stopped for supplies, but Brinley's the one who gave him a bath," Delia said.

"Brave move considering…" Vincent said.

"You mean because he's a stray?" I asked.

Vincent grunted around the bite of his sandwich.

"I thought he might be more comfortable getting bathed by me than from a stranger," I said. My relationship with the dog might only be a few hours old, but for some reason, he'd decided to bond with me, and I planned to use it to my advantage. At least until I could find him a more suitable place to live.

Myrna pulled open a bag of chips and poured them on her plate. "Leona's the one who sold me my Ziggy."

I remembered what Leona said about the increase in pet purchases since the new vet arrived in town. I'd gotten the impression the man was closer to my age and couldn't imagine Myrna being one of the women who'd wanted to impress him.

"Would you like to see a picture?" She didn't wait for me to answer before setting her plate aside so she could pull her cell out of the back pocket of her baggy shorts. She swiped her finger across the screen several times, then held the phone out to me.

It appeared that my aunt wasn't the only one who kept a pet album. I'd expected to see a cat or a dog, not the close-up photo of a black and white guinea pig.

"Isn't he adorable?" Myrna asked.

I wasn't particularly fond of creatures related to the rodent family, nor did I find keeping them as pets appealing. Myrna's attachment to Ziggy was obvious, and I didn't want to hurt her feelings. "Um, sure," I said, handing her back the phone.

"In case you were wondering, I don't have any pets or cutesy pictures to show you," Vincent said, though I hadn't thought to ask. "Tried to raise a goldfish once, but it ended belly up in its bowl after a week. I decided it might be best not to experiment with anything else."

"Sorry to hear that," I said, then popped a chip in my mouth to hide my grimace. I wasn't a fish expert either but was reasonably sure the scaly little creatures were supposed to live longer than a week. It was probably a good thing that Vincent had chosen not to be a pet owner.

"Is everyone ready to get started?" Delia asked once we'd finished our sandwiches.

Myrna and Vincent stacked their empty paper plates on the table and replied with affirmative answers.

I felt a flutter of excitement. I loved solving mysteries, but my enjoyment usually came from a book or the television. And lately, I'd been too busy with work to squeeze in much of either.

"Our visit to Leona's paid off," Delia said, then went on to share what we'd learned.

"I checked in with the network and found out that Bridget and Ellie aren't the only ones that have been robbed," Myrna said. "There have been at least three more over the last six months."

"Why haven't we heard about this before now?" Delia asked.

"These types of things don't always make it to the newspaper, but it does seem strange that there wasn't an article about it in the Promenade's monthly newsletter," Vincent said.

"Avery is usually good about reporting these kinds of things in the safety section," Delia said.

"Do you think it was because the other robberies weren't in our neighborhood?" Myrna asked.

"Even if they weren't, you'd think Carson would've mentioned them when he was questioning us," Vincent grumbled.

"Maybe the police are keeping it quiet so that news doesn't get out and hinder their investigation," I said.

"Did Leona know about the other robberies?" Vincent picked up his soda and took a swallow.

"It's possible, but she didn't say anything about them," Delia said. "She was more interested in finding out what happened with Archer."

That and trying to set me up with a date, I thought.

"It's definitely a concern, and why we need to act fast," Vincent said. "You know how narrow-minded people can be when it comes to things like this. With Carson asking questions and treating Archer like he's a suspect, how long do you think it will take for others to assume he's the one who broke into their homes?"

"Or boycott his business," Myrna said. "Remember what happened to Shelly Simpkins after the cupcake incident in her bakery? It took two weeks before anyone believed she wasn't poisoning the customers and started buying from her again."

I didn't think the two items were even closely related, but I wasn't a local and didn't have all the details, which I'm sure there were plenty, so I kept my opinions to myself.

"Vincent's right." Delia bobbed her head. "If we want to clear Archer's name, then we need to find out who's behind the thefts."

"We don't have any suspects, so where do we start?" Myrna asked.

"I think the first thing we need to do is call Zach," Vincent said.

"I agree," Myrna said.

"Me too," Delia said.

"Who's Zach?" I asked. My aunt had never mentioned the name before, so I was interested in finding out who he was and why everyone thought he'd be able to help.

"He's Vincent's sixteen-year-old grandson and also a whiz at the Crimes Galore murder mystery game we play online every week," Delia said.

"So, when you said you investigated murders, you were talking about a game?" I asked.

"Of course," Delia said. "What did you think I meant?"

"You never told me about the game before, and I haven't seen you in a while, so I had no idea."

"I know your mother thinks I'm eccentric because I don't conform to all her rules, but I don't go around provoking criminal elements." Delia winked. "At least I haven't yet."

"This will be our first challenging off-line investigation," Myrna said, then tapped her chin. "Well, except for that time we helped Clara figure out who was stealing her dog's food from the bowl she left on her back porch. Who knew seagulls could be so bold?"

"Are you saying there have been others?" I asked.

"Only a handful," Delia said.

"Nothing worth mentioning," Vincent said, then retrieved his cell phone from the back pocket of his pants. After tapping the screen several times, he placed the phone on the table.

I hoped Vincent was right, though after hearing Carson issue his warning, I had my doubts.

"Zach," Vincent said when a male voice spoke on the other end of the line.

"Hey, Granddad, how's it going?" Zach's pleasant-sounding voice was the complete opposite of Vincent's gruff one.

"Good," Vincent said. "You're on speaker with Myrna, Delia, and her niece Brinley."

"Hey, everyone," Zach said. "Since you're not alone, I'm guessing you're not calling to ask about school or girlfriends, right?"

"We wanted to get some pointers for one of the mystery scenarios we're thinking about trying," Myrna said.

"Great," Zach answered enthusiastically. "Which scenario or crime did you have in mind?"

"We wanted to try something new…say home robberies, for instance," Delia said.

These three were good. If I didn't already know what they were up to, I might have believed it was an innocent request. I hadn't paid much attention to the pen and notepad until Delia picked it up off the table, poised to take notes.

"First, I would decide if I wanted the break-in to be random or part of a series of crimes committed by a professional," Zach said. "Obviously, a random theft wouldn't provide much of a challenge, so personally, I'd go with a series of crimes."

"That's the one we need," Myrna said excitedly, then in a calmer voice, and after Delia nudged her shoulder, she added, "I mean that one does sounds like it would be more fun."

"Can you give us any pointers on things we should be searching for?" Vincent asked.

"Professionals will spend time casing their targets," Zach said. "They'll want to know what valuables are inside, so they don't waste time committing the crime."

I couldn't resist the temptation to participate and asked, "So we're looking for someone the victims have either met or know, correct?" I must have shocked the three wannabe sleuths because they simultaneously glanced in my direction.

"Absolutely," Zach said.

Myrna dropped her shoulders and sighed. "That narrows things down, but it still doesn't help identify who we're looking for."

"You're still talking about the game, right?" Zach asked, trepidation seeping into his voice. "I'm not going to regret giving you this information later, am I? You know how mom gets."

Zach sounded like an intelligent kid with good instincts. His question made it sound like he knew about his grandfather's other adventures. Maybe even approved as long as he didn't get in trouble for helping.

"I do, and you don't have anything to worry about," Vincent said. "Even if we get caught, and they torture me, your mother will never know you helped." He sounded very convincing, and if I hadn't seen the mischievous glint in his dark eyes, I would've believed him.

"Great," Zach said. "If that's all you wanted to know, then I need to get going. I still have some homework I need to finish."

"That's it… Thanks," Vincent said, then tapped the screen and disconnected the call.

"How often do you play this online mystery game Zach was talking about?" I asked, interested to learn more about the side of my aunt I had never witnessed before.

"Every week," Delia said. "We usually play at Vincent's place since his television screen is bigger than mine."

"He also has better gaming equipment," Myrna added.

"I originally bought everything for Zach's visits, but once he talked us into playing online with him, we all got hooked," Vincent said.

"What about the sleuthing thing Myrna mentioned?" I asked. "You do know that playing an online mystery game is quite a bit different and a lot safer than solving a crime in real life, right?"

Delia tsked, then said, "We've dabbled a little bit, nothing serious...or dangerous."

I'd bet their snooping was a lot more than dabbling, especially if Carson was warning them not to get involved.

Until I figured out the extent of what they planned to do with the information Zach had given them, I was going to keep an open mind and listen to their plans before deciding whether or not I should talk them out of it.

Archer seemed like a nice guy, and I couldn't blame his friends for wanting to help him. There was a good possibility they also knew the crime victims, so anything they uncovered might help them as well. As long as what they planned to do didn't get them into trouble or put them in harm's way, I didn't see how a little investigating could hurt.

Besides, I excelled at managing projects. How difficult could keeping an eye on three elderly people be? I convinced myself that by tagging along and supervising their endeavors, I'd be able to prevent any problems.

"I can't believe I'm saying this, but if we have any hope of finding out who put the bag under Archer's deck, then we need to do more research," I said.

I'd expected the approving smiles I received from Myrna and Delia. When Vincent actually grinned for the first time since I'd met him, I realized there was a softer side hidden under his gruff demeanor.

The doorbell buzzer sounded, making everyone jump

except Harley, who barked and raced from the room.

"Were you expecting someone else?" Myrna asked, glancing nervously at Delia.

"No," Delia said as she got up and hurried to follow Harley.

A few seconds later, Harley quit barking, so either Delia had gotten him to stop, or he recognized the person at the door. Curious to find out who'd arrived without being nosy and walking down the hall, I leaned forward to listen but could only hear mumbled voices.

I wasn't the only one interested. Vincent and Myrna had scooted to the edge of the sofa and had their elbows planted on their knees to keep from falling forward. The sight would have been comical if I hadn't been doing the same thing.

"Hey guys," Zoey said as she followed Delia into the room. Harley danced beside her, doing doggy pirouettes, his attention on the Styrofoam container she was carrying. "I brought some leftovers from the Bean." She set the container in the middle of the table, then flipped the lid open, exposing an assortment of croissants and a couple muffins.

"Harley," I said, snapping my fingers to draw his attention. "Those aren't for you." With a whine, he returned to his spot on the floor next to me.

"So, what did I miss?" Zoey asked.

"What makes you think you missed anything?" Vincent muttered as he grabbed a muffin.

"After listening to Archer go on for almost five minutes straight about that darned bag and what he'd do to the person who'd put it there, I realized there was a possibility that he could get blamed for the burglaries," Zoey said. "Then I thought about what would happen if he did, then I assumed the Bean would get shut down, and I'd lose the one job I really like." She took a second to inhale more air. "After that, I guessed that you guys would figure out the same thing and decide to do some of your sleuthing." She glanced at the tripod and board set up in the corner, then grinned. "I'm right, aren't I?"

I wondered if Zoey was always so explicit about sharing her thought processes.

"Yes," Myrna said, nudging Vincent until he scooted over to make room for Zoey to sit.

Delia grabbed the chair sitting next to the desk and rolled it to the other side of the couch before taking a seat. "We just got off the phone with Zach."

"Oooh, calling him was an excellent idea," Zoey said. "What did he say?"

"Here," Delia said, handing Zoey the pad with the notes she'd taken during our call. Zoey read for a few minutes, then lifted her gaze. "There's some terrific stuff here. "Do you think we should tell Archer what we're doing?"

"Not a good idea," Vincent said. "Carson is already looking into him as being a suspect. In case he gets questioned again, the less he knows, the better."

It occurred to me that Zoey, being an employee, might also be on the deputy's radar. "Did Carson question you as well?" I asked her.

Yeah," Zoey said. "He came back later and caught me when I was closing up for the day. His questions made it sound like he was still considering Archer as a suspect. That's when I decided to see if you planned to investigate and offer my assistance."

"We can always use more help," Delia said.

"Great," Zoey bounced excitedly. "Where do we start?"

"I think the first thing we should do is talk to Ellie," Myrna said. "Although she doesn't have the best memory, so I doubt she'll have any idea who knew about her valuables."

"Maybe not, but she might be able to tell us if anyone new has been in her home," Delia said.

"You mean like a service person or something?" Zoey

asked.

"That would be a great way for someone to get inside and check things out without drawing anyone's attention," I said.

"We could stop by her place tomorrow and ask her," Myrna said.

"It might look suspicious if we showed up without an invitation and started asking questions," I said. "We need to come up with a better plan if we don't want what we're doing to hit the town's main gossip line and get back to Carson or anyone else at the police station."

"Brinley's right," Vincent said.

"The thief could be anyone," Zoey said. "We definitely don't want him or her to find out what we're doing."

Delia grinned as she plucked a croissant out of the container. "I might have the perfect way for us to talk to Ellie without being conspicuous."

CHAPTER SEVEN

By the time Myrna, Delia, Vincent, Zoey, and I had finished our meeting, everyone had been assigned a task, including me. Zoey would keep an eye on things at the Bean and report back if Carson stopped by to ask any more questions. Myrna was going to nonchalantly see if her network knew of any other people living in their neighborhood that had been robbed.

Apparently, before Vincent retired, he'd had some sort of computer engineering job, so he was going to do some online recon—his words, not mine—before we all got together again. After observing his mannerisms and hearing an occasional word that regular people didn't use in conversations, I believed he may have served in the military at some point during his life.

Even if it was only temporary, owning a pet qualified me for what the group considered our first covert mission, which was extracting information from Ellie. Myrna had volunteered, but her idea of putting a tiny halter and leash on Ziggy so she could take him for a walk in the park had been vetoed. She'd gasped, her face turning a deep shade of red when Vincent told her she wouldn't be able to blend in if her guinea pig ended up as an appetizer for one of the bigger dogs during their walk.

I'd thought the same thing but would've used a gentler way to dissuade her that didn't include verbal images of her beloved pet's death. I'd learned quickly that tack wasn't one of Vincent's stronger traits, yet I found myself liking him anyway.

I had to admit that using Harley to do undercover work had been a brilliant idea, one that hadn't occurred to me until Delia told me Ellie owned a Chihuahua and took him on daily walks.

According to Myrna, many of the people, most of them retirees, liked to take their pets to the park a few blocks away from Delia's house.

If nothing else, being pulled into a mystery had me contemplating the questions Delia and I needed to ask Ellie rather than reliving the unfortunate circumstances I'd have to face once I returned home. It made falling asleep and getting some decent rest after everyone left much easier.

I wasn't excited about waking up to doggy breath with licks to my face, but it was a lot better than having my chin whacked by Luna's sharp claws. "Hey there, bud," I said, pushing Harley off my chest.

He'd had no interest in the pet bed I'd purchased for him and ran around the room and whined until I'd given in and let him on the bed. As far as sleeping partners went, a dog who liked to cuddle and didn't steal the blankets met with my approval.

I'd made sure to take Harley outside before going to bed. I didn't know the extent of his potty training, or if he'd even had any, so I checked the floor for any accidents that might have happened while I slept. "Good boy," I said and scratched his head when I didn't find any. Not wanting to push my luck, I slipped on a pair of sweats and a T-shirt. "What do you say we take a walk outside before I fix you some breakfast?"

I'd found one sandal and was on the floor on my knees

searching under the bed for the other one when I heard a noise in the hallway. Before I could retrieve my footwear, the door swung open, and Luna sauntered into the room.

"Oh no," I said, scrambling to my feet. I was glad the bed's frame wasn't high off the ground. Otherwise, when Harley barked and sailed off the mattress, he might have hurt himself. He only slowed for a few seconds when the throw rug he'd landed on skidded on the floor and bunched beneath his back legs. Nails clicked on the tiles, then faded when he reached the hallway.

I grabbed the leash, and with one foot lacking a sandal, I chased after them. When I reached the bottom of the stairs, I found the annoying furry princess perched on her usual shelf with Harley sitting on the floor, staring up at her. He swished his tail back and forth and groaned.

"What's going on in here," Delia asked as she entered the room from the kitchen. She was already dressed for the day and holding a coffee mug. The guilt I'd experienced thinking we'd woken her with our ruckus might have faded, but it didn't keep me from apologizing. "I'm so sorry."

Delia gave me a once over, her gaze briefly lingering on my feet, then smiled. "Stop worrying. They're just playing. Luna is an expert at taunting. If Harley really bothered her, we'd hear more hissing and see some claw action."

"I'm worried that your home might not withstand their playing," I said, glancing at all the nice things in the room, which included the furniture.

"At some point, we'll have to leave them alone," Delia said. "You're on vacation, and I plan to show you around town and take you to do some shopping that doesn't include sifting through toy bins for pets."

I remembered the fun I'd had searching through the toys, then holding them out to Harley to see if he approved.

"Stop fretting and go change," Delia said.

"What about Harley?" I asked. "I was about to take

him outside before Luna decided to use one of her feline gymnastic moves on the door handle again."

Delia laughed. "I think I can manage doggy potty detail." She walked over and handed me the cup in exchange for the leash. "Now go," she said, aiming me toward the stairs. "I'll make us some eggs and toast while you get dressed. After breakfast, we'll head over to the park. I can't wait to find out what Ellie has to say about the night she was robbed."

"Fine," I said, inhaling a deep whiff of the coffee's aroma before placing my barefoot on the first step. Delia's excitement was infectious and had me grinning all the way to the top of the stairs.

CHAPTER EIGHT

I was glad Harley didn't need any convincing when Delia and I prepared to leave for the park. As soon as I snapped the leash to his new collar, he eagerly hopped around, ready to go.

"How do we know for sure that Ellie is going to be in the park when we get there?" I asked once we were on the sidewalk and headed in the opposite direction of the beach. We hadn't covered that detail when we were outlining our plan the night before.

It was early in the day, and aside from the humidity, the weather was pleasant. I didn't mind the walk, but in a couple more hours, being anywhere that wasn't shaded or inside a building was going to be hot and uncomfortable.

"Going to the park is like a social imperative, even more so than attending events at the Promenade," Delia said. "Especially if you're single, more mature, and own a dog."

I couldn't believe my aunt had just insinuated that the residents in the neighborhood used the park to pick up dates. "And you know this how?" I shot her a sidelong glance, hoping that my relationship status hadn't played a part in why I'd been volunteered for this outing. I quickly dismissed the idea after remembering the majority of the people who lived in this part of town were around my aunt's age or older.

Delia wiggled her brows. "From personal experience. Myrna agrees that it's way better than online dating and much cheaper."

I closed my eyes and pinched the bridge of my nose, pushing aside the images of Myrna and my aunt hanging out in the park so they could flirt with men. "After you and Uncle Craig... I thought you didn't date anymore."

"I said I would never get married again, not that I wouldn't date." Delia stopped at a corner where two streets intersected, then looked both ways for oncoming traffic before urging me to cross to the other side with her. "Which is something you could use a little more of yourself."

"Sure, because the last time I dated a guy for longer than a week, it had worked out so well for me."

The park came into view, and Harley barked, anxiously tugging on his leash. Lush grass spread out in all directions, bordered by a moderate amount of walkways and benches. In the distance, I could see a fountain surrounded by a circular wall constructed with dark sienna bricks. There was even a sandy play area filled with various slides and equipment to keep children busy.

"You can't blame the rest of the men on the planet because what's his face decided to advance his career by dating the CEO's daughter." Delia surveyed the area where people were walking their dogs. "Quite a few nice men live here, and not all of them are my age."

"Yeah, but I'll be gone in a few days, and thanks to you and your friends, I'll be spending the rest of my time helping solve a mystery," I said, thankful for the diversion. "So, what does Ellie look like?" I added in case my change of subject didn't stop her from bringing up Carson or Jackson again.

"Like her," Delia said, then waved at a woman heading

toward us. Ellie walked slowly to keep from dragging a light brown Chihuahua who didn't seem to enjoy being on a leash. Knee-length shorts and bright-colored short-sleeved shirts appeared to be the fashion for most of the people I'd seen in the last two days. Turquoise was the prominent shade in Ellie's current outfit.

"Good morning, Delia," she said as she got closer.

"Hey, Ellie," Delia said. "I wanted to introduce you to my niece Brinley. She's visiting me for a few days."

"It's nice to meet you," Ellie said. "This is my sweet little Bruno. And who is this?" she asked, gripping her leash a little tighter and warily watching Harley as if he might make a snack out of her dog.

Besides some harmless whining followed by some sniffing, which included backsides, Harley hadn't posed a threat to Bruno. I thought about Myrna and was certain if the dog had been the only animal in the park, Ziggy would have survived an outing.

"This is Harley," I said, reaching down to pat his head, then pressing a gentle hand to his rear, encouraging him to sit.

Seeing that Harley was no longer a threat, Ellie relaxed her grip and raised her gaze to Delia. "I meant to call you yesterday, but I had a lot of things going on and forgot."

It was possible that Ellie had been busy, yet I wondered if Myrna had been right about the woman's forgetfulness.

"About what?" Delia asked.

"Carson called to tell me my things had been recovered but wouldn't say where or by whom," Ellie said. "Rumor has it that you and Brinley found a bag containing my property hidden under the deck at the Bean. Is it true?"

"Actually, it was Harley who did most of the work," I said, proudly smiling down at the dog.

"I can't thank you enough," Ellie said. "You too, Harley."

After spotting someone walking a German shepherd near the fountain, Ellie picked up Bruno and cuddled him against her chest. I kept a wary eye on the new arrival as well, intent on snatching Harley off the ground if the dog and its owner got any closer.

"I also heard that Archer is under investigation, but I don't believe it," she said.

We were supposed to be gathering new information, not sharing what we already knew. Minimizing new rumors and proving that Archer wasn't involved was a priority, and it sounded as if Ellie knew something that might help. "What makes you so sure he's innocent?" I asked.

"For one, Archer's never been to my place, and whoever broke into my house must have known Bruno would be outside while I was gone," Ellie said.

"Why do you say that?" Delia asked.

"The police found some crumbled dog biscuits in my rose bushes, which were too high off the ground for Bruno to reach. The thief must have thrown them over the back fence, then went inside and closed the doggy door to keep him in the back yard."

Delia and I shared a concerned look. After our discussion with Zach, the group had determined that the person who'd broken in must be someone the victims knew. The problem we struggled with was finding out who it could be. Maybe figuring out how and why the victims were being targeted might be helpful once we actually had some suspects.

"I'm just glad they didn't hurt my sweet little baby," Ellie said, nuzzling her dog under her chin.

"It's probably a good thing you weren't home then," Delia said.

I pondered the information Leona and Myrna had shared about the break-ins. Even more disconcerting was hearing that the most recent one occurred a few blocks away from Delia's house.

What if my aunt's place was next? What if the next time the thief broke into someone's place, the owner happened to catch them in the act? I'd read about burglaries going wrong and people getting hurt, even losing their lives trying to protect their belongings.

Normally, I'd be more than happy to let the police do their job. Now that I knew Delia's safety could be in jeopardy, I was more than a little intrigued about our discovery. I was downright concerned and willing to be more than a bystander while my aunt and her friends collected clues.

"I never miss bingo night at the Promenade," Ellie said. "I didn't have much of a winning streak and would've gone home early if Avery hadn't talked me into buying tickets for the special drawing they hold at the end of the night." She scowled. "You have to be present to win, which, of course, I didn't."

"You're talking about the Avery who is Brady's sister, right?" I asked. When Ellie flashed me a perplexed look, I added, "I met them both my first day here."

"Was Brady at the event as well?" Delia asked.

Ellie crinkled her nose as if trying to remember. "I believe he was, but I don't recall seeing him until I was getting ready to leave."

Was it possible we'd found our first suspect? Could Brady be the person responsible for the thefts? He'd seemed like such a nice guy, but I guessed a person would have to be charming to get potential targets to open up to them. He also owned a landscape maintenance business, which gave him access to a lot of properties. It wouldn't take much to observe people's habits, find out if they had pets, or do a little snooping around.

Ellie not seeing Brady until later in the evening might be a coincidence. It would be nice to have a time frame to work with, and I was curious to know when she left the event. Asking, however, would sound too nosy coming from a person she'd recently met. It wouldn't be appropriate coming from my aunt either, which had to be why she'd remained silent on the subject.

"Brinley, how long are you planning to stay?" Ellie

asked, drawing me from my musing.

"I'll be here until the end of the week." I'd detected a hint of interest that went beyond the norm of a casual conversation topic. "Why?" I didn't bother to disguise the trepidation I was feeling.

"The Promenade is having a dance. If you haven't made any plans, you should think about going." Ellie wore the same conspiratorial grin I'd seen on Myrna and Leona's faces. "It's open to the public, and some of the younger men usually attend."

Was I giving off vibes that said I was in desperate need of a boyfriend, or was matchmaking a favorite pastime for the retired women in the area? "I appreciate the invite, thanks," I said, making it sound like I was interested without making an actual commitment.

"It's too bad you didn't come for a visit during the annual volleyball competition," Ellie said, making it easy to follow her thought process. "Seeing all those bare chests and muscles..." She chuckled and fanned herself. "It's enough to make an old girl's heart flutter."

Not long after that, Ellie was on her way, and we were headed back to my aunt's place. "Admit it, this is way more fun than sitting on the beach worrying about moving to Minnesota," Delia said.

I snorted. "If your goal was to keep me distracted, you've succeeded." Unfortunately, my stay was growing shorter, and keeping me busy wasn't going to change the inevitable.

We'd barely left the park when someone called out our names. Delia and I turned in unison to see Myrna cutting across the grass to meet us, pausing to gulp in big breaths along the way.

"Do you need to sit down?" I asked, hoping she wouldn't collapse on the sidewalk and require CPR. I was certified to assist if necessary but would rather avoid it if possible. When my company had offered free training at work, I thought it might be a beneficial skill for an upcoming manager to have.

Myrna shaking her head didn't alleviate my worry, so I placed my hand on her elbow. Delia seemed just as anxious and moved to stand on Myrna's other side. "Why didn't you send me a text instead of running all the way over here?" Delia scolded.

"Phone,"—Myrna gasped—"dead."

"You mean you forgot to charge the battery again," Delia said.

"Uh-huh."

"Why didn't you drive?" I asked. The only place I'd seen so far that wasn't accessible to vehicles was the shopping area near the beach, so I assumed that most residents owned at least one car, if not more.

"Myrna's not allowed to operate any vehicles," Delia said. "There were some incidents with a couple of stop signs and a palm tree."

"Oh," I said. The way Myrna was glaring at Delia, I thought it best not to ask for any details.

As soon as Myrna's pale face gained some color and she stopped hunching over, Delia asked, "What was so urgent?"

"I found out that Corinne works for Bridget and might have done some work for Ellie," Myrna said. "Though no one in the network knew for certain."

"Who's Corinne?" I asked. "And why is that relevant?"

"She's Vincent's housekeeper," Delia said.

"And has access to their homes," I mumbled, making sense of the information. We now had two plausible suspects, which meant we needed to find a way to talk to both of them without cluing them in to what we were doing.

CHAPTER NINE

I hated to think that someone Vincent trusted enough to let into his house at least once a month could be responsible for the burglaries. I hadn't been in his home and didn't know what kind of valuables he possessed, if any. Still, if Corinne was the criminal we were searching for, he could be a potential target.

Because of Vincent's penchant for getting straight to the point without using social finesse, Myrna, Delia, and I had agreed not to tell him about his housekeeper over the phone or in-person until we could work out some sort of strategy. Personally, I thought talking to Corinne without him present might gain us the best results.

After dropping Harley off at Delia's house and walking Myrna home, my aunt and I spent a few hours doing some leisurely shopping that didn't include discussing how we would handle questioning Corinne and maybe even Brady.

It was nearing evening by the time we got back, so I decided to take Harley on one last walk before settling in for the night. So far, my vacation hadn't come close to what I'd imagined when I'd first made the decision to visit my aunt. Between the sleuthing quest and taking care of Harley, I'd gotten in more exercise than I'd expected. I'd been so busy that I hadn't had a chance to contemplate the dramatic change my future would be taking or how disappointed I was at the prospect.

Instead, I'd been focusing on what I'd learned from my first official day of investigating. Continuing with the belief that Archer wasn't the thief left me with several unanswered questions. The main one whirling through my mind centered on the Bean and why the deck had been chosen as a hiding place. Unless the burglar was afraid the police had discovered their identity, wouldn't it have been wiser to hide the goods someplace that wasn't so public. And, more importantly, why would they be in an area near the beach and filled with businesses?

According to Delia, residential neighborhoods stretched out on both sides of the shopping area. Ellie's home wasn't that far from my aunt's house and nowhere near the Bean or the side of the building where I'd found the bag.

When I reached the sidewalk that would either take us to the park or the Bean, depending on the direction, I stopped and glanced down at Harley. "How do you feel about taking a stroll along the beach? There's something I'd like to check out."

Logically, I knew the dog didn't really understand the question, but his responding bark made me feel like he had. "Okay then, let's go."

I was anxious to reach my destination, check out the block on the other side of the Bean, and return to Delia's house before it got dark. Harley must have sensed my anxiety because his short legs worked faster the closer we got to Archer's place.

The shops along the main street were still open, but the coffee bar was closed. The only visible lights near the building came from an exterior outlet near the front door and several more mounted on the wall beside the deck.

Harley and I continued to the side of the building where we'd found the bag. Archer hadn't wasted any time cleaning up the area and making it presentable. The dirt in the bed had been evened out, leaving an empty spot. The plants Harley had dug up and discarded were gone.

I stepped into the bed to get a better look at the panel, unsure what I hoped to find. A blaring clue would've been nice. Instead, I noticed that the loose boards had been restored, and it looked like a few more screws had been added to keep them in place. Anyone who accessed it now would have to be toting some kind of tool.

"Excuse me, miss," a male voice, deep and familiar, called from behind me.

I squeaked and spun around so fast that I would've fallen backward into the bushes if Carson hadn't caught me by the arm.

Some watchdog Harley had turned out to be. He hadn't even barked to let me know that we weren't alone. The dog wagged his tail, seemingly more interested in getting Carson to give him some attention, which surprisingly the man did before focusing his scrutinizing frown back on me.

"Brinley, what do you think you're doing?" he asked before removing his hand.

He'd changed out of his uniform and was wearing shorts, a T-shirt, and slip-on shoes without socks. If he wasn't on duty, I was curious to know what he was doing hanging out near the Bean.

I returned his intense gaze with a glare of my own. I wasn't about to tell him the real reason he'd found me examining the panel. "I was walking my dog. That's not a crime, is it?" I asked a little too defensively.

"No, but trespassing is?" Carson crossed his arms but didn't move.

I glanced down at my feet and the prints I'd left in the dirt, then to the place where he was standing. He hadn't stepped over the ornate border like I had, but he'd moved close to its edge. "Technically, if leaving the sidewalk is considered breaking the law, then I'm pretty sure I'm not the only guilty party here." I wiggled my finger at his feet.

"Fine," he groaned, then stepped aside and followed me back to the sidewalk.

I still wanted to explore the neighboring blocks, but I didn't want to do it while being scrutinized by the infuriating deputy. I'd hoped by ignoring Carson that he'd leave and go about his business. Instead, he stayed where he was, letting the silence build between us, which only made my anxiety worse. When he did finally speak, I fought hard not to jump. "Your aunt and her friends are doing what I specifically asked them not to, aren't they?"

I wasn't good at acting clueless but figured I'd give it a try anyway. "I'm just visiting and have no idea what it is they're not supposed to be doing," I said.

"So, I guess it's only you who's meddling in my investigation, then," he said.

"How is walking my dog meddling?" I'd thought about batting my eyelashes to appear innocent, but without any practice, I wasn't sure if I'd be able to pull it off.

Rather than call my bluff and issue another warning, he grinned and shook his head. "You are definitely related to Delia."

"Thanks," I said, though I didn't think he'd meant it as a compliment. There weren't any homes close by, so I didn't think him showing up at the Bean had been a coincidence. Since he obviously wasn't going to leave any time soon, I decided to make the most of an annoying situation. "Do you always make a habit of stalking visitors?"

"Stalking? What...no." He ran his hand through his short dark strands. "Maybe, like you, I was out for a leisurely walk."

"Uh-huh," I said, quirking a brow to let him know his attempt to derail me wasn't working. I at least had a dog I could use as a prop, but thought he wouldn't appreciate me pointing that out to him.

Working in a managerial role had given me plenty of

experience dealing with all kinds of situations, not to mention a good amount of my own personal determination. "Delia and her friends are convinced that you think Archer's guilty. Were you staking out the Bean, hoping to catch him hiding another bag?"

"I suppose they're not going to leave it alone until they hear otherwise, are they?" Carson muttered in frustration, and I expected him to start grinding his teeth any second now.

I shrugged. At this point, I didn't think the three of them would walk away from solving the mystery even if they knew Archer wouldn't be blamed.

"Look, I've known Archer since I was a boy," Carson said. "The only crime he's ever been guilty of is serving decadent breakfast items."

"So why all the questioning and making everyone think you believe he did it?" I asked before the answer dawned on me. "You're using him as a decoy, hoping you'll trap the real thief."

"Since this is an ongoing investigation, and I'm not supposed to share information with civilians, I won't confirm or deny anything."

"I understand," I said. "Harley and I will do our best not to blow your cover."

He grinned. "Delia did say you were intelligent."

I cringed, remembering Myrna's, Leona's, and my aunt's attempts at improving my love life. Thinking about the number of single men Delia might have shared her opinions of me with before I'd arrived was making my head hurt. "Do I want to know what else my aunt told you about me, or if she handed out a resume?"

Carson chuckled. "Don't worry, I didn't get a flyer, and she didn't tell me anything that would tarnish your reputation...or land you in jail," he said with a wink. "I might have to amend that last part if I find you loitering in anyone else's landscaping."

I wasn't going to be around long enough to develop a

reputation. At least I hoped I wasn't. "Got it. No more playing in the dirt." I glanced at Harley, who was happily sniffing the ground. "Though I can't make any promises about my dog."

"Fair enough," Carson said. "Now, can you make it back to Delia's on your own, or do you need a police escort?"

Daylight was quickly fading, so doing any more exploring would have to wait. "I think I can make it without any assistance, but thanks for the offer." I headed in the direction of my aunt's house, stopping long enough to look over my shoulder to see Carson still watching me. With a wave, he finally turned and went in the opposite direction.

The return journey passed quickly, my thoughts consumed with the new information I'd gleaned from Carson. As soon as I entered the house and found Delia in the kitchen, I said, "I think we need to call an emergency meeting."

CHAPTER TEN

While I replaced Harley's water and filled the other bowl with dog food, Delia called Myrna, Vincent, and Zoey. It didn't take long for them to arrive and the three of us to migrate to my aunt's office to discuss what I'd learned from my encounter with Carson.

The board Vincent had brought the last time we'd met was still sitting in the corner. The notes Delia had taken during our call with Zach were now scrawled in a list along the smooth white surface. The word "Suspects" had been added along with Brady's name. Corinne was still a possibility, but my aunt and I decided to wait to write it on the board.

I assumed Vincent had already done his research. He'd brought a laptop and had it balanced on his lap. Without any food to draw his attention, Harley seemed content to lay on the floor near my chair.

Instead of taking a seat on the couch with Myrna and Vincent, Zoey knelt on the floor, then unfolded a colorful pamphlet and spread it out in the center of the coffee table. "I watch a lot of crime shows, and sometimes the cops need to pinpoint a location, so I thought this might help."

"What is it?" I asked, scooting to the edge of my chair to get a better look.

"It's a map of the area," Zoey said. "They hand them out to visitors and potential home buyers at the Promenade."

"Smart thinking," Delia said, making Zoey blush.

Having a visual of the town meant I'd be able to see what was in the area on the other side of Archer's place without having to make a trip and risk being caught by Carson again. The map didn't show each residential house like an aerial view did, but it had all the streets and squares for important landmarks, including the main shopping area and the Bean. "No kidding," I said, picking up the pen Delia had used during our last meeting. "Do you mind if we mark on it?"

"Not at all," Zoey said. "I have a membership, so I can always pick up another one."

"Good." I handed the pen to Myrna. "Can you put an x in the general location of Ellie's and Bridget's house, and any of the other people you heard had been robbed?

"Sure." Myrna squinted through the thick lenses of her glasses, then made three marks on the paper. "Ellie lives here." She tapped one of the marks, then moved on to the next. "And Bridget."

I noticed the name of the street Delia lived on and its proximity to Ellie's place, which was only a few blocks away.

"This is the park." Myrna tapped a small green area not far from my aunt's home. "And this is the Promenade."

"Who lives there?" Delia asked, pointing at the mark situated in the area I didn't get to explore.

"That's Clara Jessop's place," Myrna said. I've met her a couple of times, but don't know her all that well.

I scanned the rest of the map until I found the Bean. "What's this?" I asked, placing my fingertip on the large spot shaded in brown to the right of it.

"That's the visitor parking area for the beach and main

street shopping," Myrna said. "Tourists and most everyone who doesn't want to walk, parks their vehicles there."

"Now that you're up to date on local information, would you mind telling us why you called a special meeting?" Vincent asked, his grumble laced with excitement.

"Given that Ellie's house and the Bean aren't located near each other, I thought it was strange that someone would pick Archer's place to hide stolen goods," I said. "It would've made more sense if the bag we found had contained items from this robbery instead." I tapped the mark representing Clara's home. "When I took Harley for his walk, I decided to stroll along the beach and see if I could find a clue or gain some insight."

"Did you find something helpful?" Myrna asked.

"The only thing I found was Carson lurking around."

"Carson?" Vincent asked. "What was he doing there?"

"He wouldn't tell me," I said. "He was more interested in finding out why I was there and if you guys were doing any investigating after he told you not to."

Delia frowned. "You didn't…"

"No, I didn't say anything, but I don't think he believed me."

"Does that means he'll be keeping a closer eye on our activities?" Zoey asked, no doubt afraid the deputy would be by to question her again.

"More than likely," I said, remembering Carson's persistence. He was going out of his way to catch the thieves, so I wouldn't put it past him to keep track of our movements as well.

"It just means we'll have to be more careful," Delia said, getting everyone to nod in agreement.

"Carson didn't come right out and say it, but I don't believe he thinks Archer is guilty either," I said. "I think he was hanging around the Bean to see if the real thief would return."

"I'm not sure why he'd bother," Zoey said. "The way

gossip travels around town, the thief has to know Carson already confiscated the bag."

"Even so, we still need to figure out why Archer was targeted in the first place," I said.

"I was thinking," Zoey said. "Wouldn't the thief need a car parked somewhere close in case the owner came home early and they needed to make a quick getaway?"

Delia snapped her fingers. "If it was someone people in the neighborhood knew, then they wouldn't risk leaving their vehicle on the street to be recognized."

"They could be using the lot near the Bean," Vincent said. "It's empty most nights, isn't it?" He glanced at Zoey.

"Yeah, unless some teenagers decide to hang out on the beach or someone's booked a special event."

I did my best thinking when I paced, so I pushed out of my chair and moved to the area behind Zoey. As soon as I took a few steps, Harley got up to walk with me. After running what Zoey had said through my mind, I turned and faced the group. "This is purely speculation, but what if the person who robbed Ellie parked in the lot, but people were hanging around when he or she got there. Most people wouldn't give a person heading to their vehicle much thought, but a person carrying a bulky bag…"

"Would definitely be noticed," Zoey said, shifting sideways and finishing for me.

"If you're correct, then the thief needed a place to hide the bag," Delia said. "The Bean was close, and people rarely walk along that side of the building. The bushes would've been enough to conceal the bag until they could come back and get it."

"They must have found the loose panels and decided to put it underneath the deck instead," Vincent said.

"It would be the perfect way not to get caught." Myrna clasped her hands in her lap and squirmed like an excited child.

"Though I'll bet the thief never anticipated an

inquisitive pup to uncover the goods," I said, reaching down to give Harley a pat.

"The theory sounds plausible, but there's no way to prove whether or not you're right," Vincent said.

Delia puffed out an exasperated breath. "Which means Archer still looks guilty, and we're back to finding the person responsible."

"What if there was more to the break-ins than we originally believed?" Vincent asked.

"Like what?" I stepped around Harley and returned to my seat.

"I got to thinking about Zach's comment." Vincent ran his fingers across the laptop's keyboard at an impressive speed.

"Which one?" I asked, glancing at the board and the list his grandson had provided us.

"That a professional thief, someone who's made a career out of stealing, might be behind the robberies." Vincent raised his gaze, a hint of a grin forming at the end of his lips.

"Did you find something?" Delia asked, leaning toward the couch, trying to get a glimpse of the computer screen.

"Maybe," Vincent said, hitting the enter key. "In all the years I've lived here, our neighborhood has never had this sort of problem, so I began to wonder if our town was the only place the thief had been stealing. Then I remembered reading an article about similar robberies that occurred in a retirement area up the coast from us."

"Vincent is a news buff and has online subscriptions to several newspapers throughout the state," Myrna said for my benefit.

"The reason those thefts made the news was because a home owner died during one of the break-ins," Vincent said, turning the computer around so we could see the screen.

Myrna pressed her hand to her chest. "Are you saying they killed someone on purpose?"

"Not according to the article. The police think the owner came home early and interrupted the robbery."

The fear of the same thing happening to my aunt was why I wanted the thief caught before returning home. Knowing how easily it could happen increased my determination to help the group solve the mystery.

I scanned the article, then looked up at Vincent. "Are you saying you think there's a connection between those robberies and the ones occurring here?"

"Analyzing data was part of my job before I retired," Vincent said. "After noticing a two-month gap in the timeline between when those thefts stopped hitting the news and we started having activity here, I'd have to say yes."

I glanced at the date on the screen, then did a quick calculation in my head. "It sounds like we're looking for someone who moved to the area approximately eight months ago, give or take."

"Yep," Vincent said.

"If we're still searching for someone who can easily access a home or gain information about belongings, then who is new to the area and fits those parameters?" I asked.

"Brady Noonan," Delia said.

"What about his sister Avery?" I asked, thinking that the two might have relocated at the same time.

"She's been here for a couple of years," Myrna said. "Brady moved here sometime this year, but I can't remember when. Rumor has it he had money problems, and that's why he's staying with his sister."

We already had Brady on our suspect list, and it appeared we might also have a motive. Even if he did have financial issues, it didn't mean he'd resorted to a life of crime. I didn't want to single him out until I could prove it one way or the other. "Anyone else?" I asked.

"Owen Metcalf and his wife," Myrna said. "You met him at the Bean."

"He's the guy who came out here to take over

managing the Promenade, right?" I asked.

Myrna frowned. "I still think Benjamin should have gotten the promotion. Everyone loves him, and he's a lot nicer to the people living in the community than that grump Owen."

Before Myrna could continue her disgruntled rant, Delia interceded. "That gives us three possibilities."

"Actually, four," I said. "I don't think we should rule Avery out yet. I know you said she's been here longer, but thefts are also committed by women. What if she's helping her brother?"

"Oooh, that's a good point," Zoey said.

"I don't think we can rule anyone out until we gather more information and confirm alibis," Vincent said.

"I agree, so what do we do now?" Delia asked.

I wasn't sure why everyone was looking at me as if I held all the answers. My aunt and her friends were the ones with some investigating experience, not to mention all the hours they'd logged playing their mystery game.

I thought about the conversation I'd had with Carson and how I'd brought up the subject of Archer being a decoy. He hadn't confirmed that I was right, nor did he tell me I was wrong. Did he know about the other robberies and had made the same assumption we had? Was it possible he'd developed a list of suspects and had them under surveillance? "I'm curious. Has Carson always attended the events hosted at the Promenade?"

"He used to show up once in a while, but lately he's been hanging around a lot more," Delia said. "Which isn't a bad thing since he's such a good dancer."

"And easy on the eyes," Zoey said.

"Yeah," Myrna agreed with an appreciative sigh.

Vincent rolled his eyes at the three women. "Why do you ask?"

"What if he started going to more functions because he thinks the thief is someone who either attends the activities or works at the Promenade?" I asked.

"That totally makes sense," Zoey said.

"It's too bad we can't ask him what he knows," Myrna said.

I grinned at the group. "No, but what's to stop us from visiting the Promenade and doing a little inquiring of our own?"

CHAPTER ELEVEN

Zoey had to work, so Delia, Myrna, and I made the trip to the Promenade. Our latest sleuthing endeavor to gather clues required social finesse, so we'd unanimously agreed that Vincent's time would be better spent doing more research. Instead of arguing, he'd actually seemed relieved to be left behind.

We decided to use Ellie's suggestion of signing up for the upcoming dance as our cover. Actually, attending the event would depend on what we discovered from our outing. I wouldn't mind spending time dancing. It would be a great way to burn off some unwanted stress and hopefully enjoy what remained of my vacation.

Unfortunately, the closer it got to the end of my stay, the more I worried about leaving my aunt. My anxiety had risen even more after reading the article about the man who'd been killed in his own home as a result of a break-in.

After seeing Myrna almost pass out from her jaunt the day before, I decided driving would be better than walking to the community center's office. Since we weren't going to be gone long, and I was fairly certain I could trust Harley not to destroy the inside of Delia's home or eat her cat, I left him behind.

Our destination was easy to find. A tall, curved sign with the words "Pelican Promenade" was situated inside a lushly landscaped area to the left of the paved entrance. The business office was a single-story building trimmed in white and painted the same slate gray as the sign.

"That's the activity center over there," Delia said, pointing at a much larger building located on the opposite side of the lot.

"Benjamin's not in his office right now, so we can investigate without him getting suspicious and asking questions. Even so, we shouldn't dally," Myrna said, hastening her steps as we crossed the parking lot.

I was impressed at her forethought but concerned about what she'd done to make things less conspicuous for us. "How do you know he's not going to be here?" I asked.

Myrna slowed for a second and shrugged. "He might have gotten an anonymous call about a gopher invasion a few blocks away."

"Seriously," Delia said. "I didn't know we even had a gopher problem in town."

"We don't," Myrna giggled. "But I don't think my nephew knows that."

Hanging out with Myrna was entertaining. I clamped my lips to hide my amusement, then held the door open for the two women to go in ahead of me.

The interior was spacious and welcoming. Light tan ceramic tile covered the floor of the lobby area and ended near a wooden reception counter. Patterned print carpet spanned the remainder of the room. Two of the back walls contained offices, each with a large glass panel that provided an ample view of the entire area. Avery sat behind a desk in the office closest to the reception counter.

As soon as the chime on the main door rang, she looked up from whatever she was working on and smiled at us. She pulled on a light suit jacket as she rose from her chair, then came out to greet us. "Good morning. How's everyone doing today?"

"This is the quietest I've ever seen this place," Myrna said, glancing around at the empty room. "Especially with a dance scheduled for tomorrow night."

"It's still early," Avery said. "I give it another hour before all the last-minute sign-ups start arriving." She smiled and walked over to the counter. "Is that why you're here?"

"It is," Delia said.

"Great." Avery stepped up to a computer system sitting off to the right. "Then let's get you registered."

"I don't know if I should go," Myrna said, feigning trepidation.

"Why not?" Avery paused with her hands over the keyboard.

"After hearing about Ellie's robbery, I'm a little worried about going anywhere at night," Myrna said, launching into the fabricated story we'd come up with on our drive over. "What if my place is next?"

"Why would you think that?" I'd been studying Avery's reaction, searching for any hint of deceit, but so far, her responses seemed genuine.

"My grandmother left me a diamond necklace when she passed. I had it appraised, and it's worth a small fortune. I'm pretty sure I could take a world cruise and still have money left over if I ever decided to sell it."

Myrna's overly done exaggeration had me holding back a gasp. The part about the cruise hadn't been in our original story. Delia had told her friend to make the necklace appear valuable, not make it sound like it was a piece fit for royalty.

Avery's dark eyes widened. "Didn't you get it insured?"

"Of course, I did, but it's an heirloom, and the sentimental value alone makes it irreplaceable." Myrna placed her hands on the end of the counter and sighed.

"Brinley suggested I have a safe installed in my home."

"It's probably not a bad idea," Avery said. "If you don't want to go with a safe, you might consider getting a deposit box at the bank."

When it came to dramatics, I always thought my mother should win an award. After watching Myrna's performance, I realized my mother was only an amateur.

"I like Avery's suggestion better," I said. "A bank would have way more security than your house."

"Did I hear you say something about needing security?" Owen said as he walked out of an office several doors down from Avery's.

I hadn't realized how much voices carried inside the building until he mentioned overhearing part of our conversation, which actually worked to our advantage since he was one of our suspects.

"Good morning, Owen," Delia said.

He forced a smile and returned her greeting, then pinned Myrna with a look that said he expected an answer. I'd only seen the man twice but was starting to agree with Myrna about his lack of social skills.

"Yes, I completely forgot that I'd hidden my grandmother's necklace in a shoebox on the top shelf of my closet." Myrna touched her chin and shook her head as if being forgetful was normal for her. "I hadn't given it any thought until I heard about what happened at Archer's place." She gave Owen's arm a pat. "You know...the bag Brinley found with Ellie's belongings in it."

He tensed and wrinkled his nose. "I heard about that, and I'm sure Carson will find the person responsible." Owen tugged on his collar as if it had started choking him. I couldn't tell if it was us or the topic we were discussing that made him uncomfortable.

"Do you happen to know if Corinne is home today?" Delia asked. "I was hoping to call and stop by so I can introduce her to Brinley."

"She's not there," Owen said, his tone brusque. "But if

you feel like sticking around, she's supposed to be here in about ten minutes or so."

"I don't mind waiting at all," Delia smiled at Myrna and me. "Do you?"

"No," I said.

"Me neither," Myrna said.

"Actually, Corinne arrived a little bit ago. She's in the break room getting some coffee," Avery said. "I'll go get her for you." Before any of us could thank her, she spun and took off for the hallway at the other end of the room.

"I'll let you get back to business then." Owen dismissed us with a tip of his head and returned to his office.

"Why did you ask Owen about Corinne?" I asked once he was out of sight, though this time, I remembered to keep my voice low when I spoke.

"Corinne is Owen's wife," Delia said. "I'm sorry. I thought I told you."

"It's not a problem, but it does make me wonder why she'd choose housekeeping as a profession." I tucked my hands in my pockets. "Doesn't the manager's job pay well?" I figured Myrna would know because of her nephew's position.

"According to Benjamin, it does," Myrna said.

"I don't know if they need the money or if Corinne does the work to get out of the house." Delia glanced toward Owen's office. "Maybe she needs something to do to get away from her husband."

"We could always ask her." Myrna smirked when she saw Avery reappear with an older woman whose outfit spoke of money and fashion, not something worn to clean houses.

Delia gave Myrna a warning poke with her elbow. "No. We can't, so don't even think about it."

After meeting Corinne, who, personality-wise, was the complete opposite of Owen, I was ready to agree with my aunt's assumption about her reason for becoming a part-time housekeeper.

"You are planning on attending the dance, aren't you?" Corinne asked.

"Myrna's concerned about an heirloom issue," Avery said as she entered data into the computer. Realizing she'd shared personal information without thinking, she jerked her head away from the screen, red blossoming on her face. "Oh, I'm sorry, I didn't mean to…"

"It's okay," Myrna said, doing a good job of hiding the fact that we wanted Corinne to have the information.

"What kind of issue?" Corinne asked, intrigued.

Myrna spent the next few minutes repeating what she'd already told Avery.

"Your necklace is probably safe for the moment, but I agree with finding a better place to keep it," Corinne said. "But I don't think you should let that keep you from going to the dance."

"You're probably right," Myrna said. "Avery, go ahead and sign me up as well."

"Wonderful," Avery said, and within minutes, had the three of us registered and on our way.

I couldn't believe our luck when we'd stepped outside and found Brady lifting the tailgate on his truck. He pulled off a pair of work gloves and stuck them in the back pocket of his shorts.

"Ladies," Brady said, flashing us a wide smile. "I hope you signed up for the dance."

"Sure did," Myrna said. "Are you going to be there?"

"Wouldn't miss it." He took a few steps backward, the door to the reception area his intended target. "Make sure you save a couple for me." He winked in my direction, and with a friendly wave, disappeared inside.

"Don't you think we should have told him about the necklace?" Myrna asked after climbing in the back seat of my car.

"I have a feeling Avery will take care of that for us," I said, remembering how eager she was to share the information with Corinne. I snapped on my seat belt, then turned the ignition. As I drove out of the complex, a feeling of satisfaction rushed through my system. We still didn't know who was behind the thefts or how they were selecting their targets, but as far as tracking down potential suspects and setting our plan into action went, our endeavors were going a lot better than I'd expected.

CHAPTER TWELVE

After checking in for the dance, I scoped out the large room, searching for our suspects. I took a moment to appreciate the Hawaiian-themed decorations and the elegant buffet tables situated along the back wall.

"Did Avery do all this?" I asked Delia, who'd taken the lead ahead of Myrna, Zoey, and me.

"She may have had help from some of the staff, but she usually does most of the work herself," she said.

A portable dance floor had been placed in the center of the room, with several couples already swaying to the beat of the DJ's current selection. Small groups of people, also dressed in nice casual wear, had gathered either to stand or sit at one of the smaller tables covered with colorful cloths positioned around the dance area perimeter.

"Is everyone clear on what you're supposed to do?" I asked, taking the leadership role I'd been volunteered for by the rest of the group seriously.

I received affirmative responses and nods from the three women. Vincent had gladly signed up to stay behind and watch Myrna's place. He'd insisted on keeping Harley with him, stating that my dog would provide an excellent cover for any recon. I trusted him to look after my pet, but

I worried when he told us his plans for testing his new binoculars. I hoped bailing him out of jail wouldn't be part of the night's events.

We didn't have any fancy ear gadgets to communicate with one another, but we did have our cell phones programmed with each other's numbers, including one for the police department. Although it took several reminders from Delia, even Myrna's phone was charged and ready to go.

I'd worn a sleeveless summer top with a floral print and a black shirt. Instead of the dress heels I would've normally worn with the outfit, I'd gone with half-inch flats in case moving quickly was required. Not that chasing a thief was on my itinerary for the evening, but I wanted to be prepared anyway. If things went the way we'd planned, we'd track the culprit, then call the police and let them handle things.

We hadn't moved very far from the entrance and I was afraid we'd gain attention if we continued standing in the same spot staring at everyone else. "We should probably split up," I said. "Try to act natural," I added as an afterthought.

"Great idea," Zoey said. "If you don't mind, I'll catch up with you guys later." She took off toward a group of women around her same age on the other side of the room. From the excited shrills and hugging, I was sure they were some of Zoey's close friends.

The upbeat music was hard to resist, and I longed to spend some time on the dance floor. My main goal was keeping an eye on our suspects, so I wouldn't be going out of my way to find a dance partner. It didn't mean I'd be rude and turn down an offer.

"What do you say we get some snacks?" Delia asked, motioning us toward the buffet tables.

We were halfway to our destination when a silver-haired man stepped away from a nearby group. "Hey, Myrna, feel like taking a spin?" I hoped he meant around the floor and not in his car.

"Absolutely." Myrna took the man's offered hand, and when he wasn't looking, grinned at Delia and me, then wiggled her brow.

"Don't go too far, Delia," he called over his shoulder. "I'll be back to get you later."

I was relieved that he hadn't bothered to ask who I was or include me in his future dance plans.

"Okay," my aunt said, then placed her hand on my back and urged me to move away from the spinning couples. "Robert is a sweet enough guy, but he has two left feet when it comes to dancing. If you do agree to go out on the floor with him, be careful, or your toes will take a beating."

Under the guise of enjoying some incredible chocolate iced brownies, which didn't take much effort, I went back to scanning faces. So far, Avery and Owen were the only ones I'd spotted out of the four people on our suspect list.

Avery was working her way around the room, smiling and speaking to everyone she came across. Owen wasn't exactly mingling, more like holding down a spot at the other end of the buffet tables and stiffly greeting anyone who got near him. I'd gotten my fill of the man the last time we'd spoken. I didn't feel obliged to speak with him again, but I was going to monitor his movements.

"Ladies," Archer said, arriving at the table a few minutes after we did. "How's the vacation going?"

"Delia's been keeping me busy," I said, not letting on that most of my time was spent in pursuit of a criminal.

"No doubt," Archer laughed. After a few more minutes of pleasantries about nothing important, he asked, "Do you mind if I steal your aunt?"

"No, go right ahead," I said.

Delia flashed me an are-you-sure look, which I answered with a subtle tip of my head. We might be undercover, but I didn't want to stop my aunt and new friends from having fun.

With Myrna still out on the floor with Robert and Zoey bouncing to the musical beats with her friends, I was free to indulge in another brownie. My so-called surveillance was interrupted when I spotted Brady heading toward me. He smiled and walked with a confident stride like a person with a mission. A mission, I was afraid, appeared to be me.

Even if I wasn't leaving tomorrow, I had no interest in getting to know him on a personal level. I was, however, pondering a way to extract more information to prove whether or not he was our thief.

When Brady was about fifteen feet away, he paused and frowned, then did a quick about-face. I was relieved, annoyed, and bewildered at the same time. I had no idea what I'd done that would cause him to change his mind.

"It appears I may have cost you a dance," Carson said from behind me.

My stomach fluttered, not from being surprised by his arrival but from his nearness. Carson seemed to make every outfit he wore look good. I had no doubt that the dark pants and button-down shirt he'd donned for the event would have quite a few women drooling. At the moment, I was doing my best not to be one of them.

"What makes you say that?" I asked.

He reached around me to snatch a chocolate-chip cookie off one of the plates on the table. "Let's just say Mr. Noonan and I have crossed paths over some minor altercations, and he has a tendency to stay clear of me."

"I see," I said, wondering if he'd purposely meant to run Brady off or if I'd imagined it.

Carson finished chewing a bite of the cookie, then asked, "Where's Vincent tonight?" He must have been here long enough to see Myrna and Delia. Since he hadn't asked about Zoey, I figured he wasn't aware that she was helping us, and I wasn't about to tell him.

"My aunt's cat and Harley have a strained relationship, so he volunteered for doggy babysitting duty so I could attend the dance." It was mostly true, so the guilt I felt was minimal.

"That was nice of him," Carson said, a hint of skepticism in his tone.

I assumed once Carson finished his cookie he'd move on, but he seemed content to grab another one and remain where he was.

I had yet to get a visual on Corinne, and when I glanced at the place where I'd last seen Owen, he was gone. I strained to remain calm, not frantically move around the room and search for our two missing suspects.

I felt a tingle near the top of my leg and didn't get a chance to ponder what I should do next. Afraid that I wouldn't hear the ring tone over the music, I'd programmed my phone to vibrate and kept it in the pocket of my skirt.

I pulled out my phone, careful to shield the message on the screen from Carson. The text, which had also been sent to Myrna, Delia, and Zoey, was from Vincent and read, *Intruder spotted. Need backup.*

My pulse quickened, and I didn't need to scan the room to know my aunt and friends would be heading for the parking lot. Since I had a member of local law enforcement literally within reach, I tucked the phone in my pocket as I spun to face Carson again. "How badly do you want to catch your thief?"

"Brinley," he said and scowled.

I grabbed his hand and pulled him toward the front door. "You can lecture me later."

CHAPTER THIRTEEN

When Carson and I reached the Promenade's parking lot, he insisted that Myrna and Zoey ride with Delia in my car. I ended up riding with him in his truck, so I could explain what was going on before we reached Vincent's place.

He'd asked a lot of questions and done quite a bit of grumbling along the way. He'd been furious when he learned the extent of our investigation, but I had to give him points for not losing his temper completely.

The others arrived right before us and parked in the driveway, leaving a spot on the street in front of Vincent's house for Carson's vehicle. Myrna was the first one to hit the sidewalk and hurry to the porch. It wasn't exactly a sprint, but she was moving faster than she had the day she tracked down Delia and me in the park.

"Vincent," she hollered, not bothering to knock before opening the door.

By the time the rest of us stepped into the foyer, Myrna was emerging from the kitchen. "Ziggy's okay, but I can't find Vincent."

Tension had been my constant companion since I'd received Vincent's text. It had gotten considerably worse when he hadn't been at the door to greet us. "You don't think he went to your place by himself, do you?" I knew the answer before the question left my mouth. I'd thought about calling him, then quickly rejected the idea. If he had followed the thief to Myrna's, I didn't want to risk the ring on his cell phone announcing his presence to the intruder.

Myrna rubbed her bare arms. "He does have a key for emergency purposes."

Carson reacted to the news by pinning each of us with his intense dark gaze. "I need you four to stay here while I go check it out."

"Like heck, we will," Delia said, pushing past him before he could stop her. Myrna and Zoey moved to follow after her.

Realizing it was a losing battle to argue with a group of determined women, Carson groaned and rushed to get ahead of my aunt. I might have been more sympathetic to the deputy's dilemma if I wasn't more concerned about Vincent. Because if we were right about the recent thefts being connected to ones he'd found in the newspaper article, then the risk of losing his life was a strong possibility.

Myrna's place was three houses down and across the street. On our way there, Carson made a call, giving whoever answered our location and telling them he needed backup. Most of the neighboring homes were dark, the occupants still out or retired for the night. Luckily, there was a street lamp close by, which provided enough light for us to see where we were going.

The porch light should have been the only light on, but a soft glow appeared around the edges of the blind in a corner room on the right.

Myrna stopped on the sidewalk to glare at her house. "What kind of thief turns on the lights?"

"I'm about to find out," Carson said, holding out his hand for the keys Myrna clasped in her fist. Instead of entering through the front door, he circled along the side of the building. The rest of us followed him into the backyard. Before inserting the key in the lock, he tried sliding the patio door and found that it moved easily.

A good thief could break into a home without causing much damage. Had this been the entrance he or she had used? I hadn't seen Corinne or Owen before we'd left the dance, so I still had no idea who was doing the stealing. I couldn't rule out a husband and wife team, but my instincts were leaning toward Owen. Maybe it was wishful thinking because I didn't want to believe that Corinne could be involved.

Carson didn't need to tell us to remain quiet. Vincent was our friend, and we were well aware of the risks. We weren't, however, going to wait on Myrna's patio while he went to check things out inside. I was relieved when he didn't bother trying, and I was even happier when I heard Harley's barks echoing from the other end of the house.

Carson took the lead, the rest of us staying a few feet behind him. Movement at the other end of the hallway caused him to put out his arm, forcing us to stop. When Vincent stepped out of the lighted room, Carson groaned, sounding more relieved than irritated.

"It's about time you got here," Vincent said, grinning as he moved away from the doorway so we could all enter Myrna's bedroom while keeping a tight grip on Harley's leash.

"Unbelievable," Carson muttered, rubbing his nape as his gaze swept across the room.

Myrna clapped her hands and bounced from one foot to the other. "I would have to say that operation mousetrap was a success, wouldn't you?"

"I'll say," Delia said, a satisfied smile forming on her lips.

"Wow." Zoey shifted her surprised gaze to Myrna. "I can't believe your idea actually worked."

I'd had my own reservations when Myrna had first made the suggestion, but since we couldn't come up with an alternative, I'd supported her plan. After getting a good look at the inside of the room, I was glad I had.

Owen was standing in a corner with his back pressed to the wall. Other than his head and hands, his entire body was covered in black, even the knit face mask he clutched in his hand. Two mouse traps clung to the loose fabric of his pants, and quite a few more were scattered on the carpet near the entrance to the closet.

The shoe box Delia had placed underneath a stack of blankets was also lying nearby, with the lid a few feet away. The traps were meant to be a distraction, and we hadn't wanted them to be seen until it was too late. We figured the thief would resort to using a flashlight, but in case we were wrong, we decided to minimize the risk by having Zoey remove the bulb in the closet.

The way Harley was barking and hopping back and forth reminded me of a life-size children's wind-up toy. If Owen made the slightest movement, my dog's snarls turned feral. I couldn't have been prouder of the little furball.

"Exactly how many traps did you set?" Carson asked, the shock of what we'd done finally wearing off.

Myrna snickered. "Let's just say that anyone with a rodent problem will have to wait for all the stores in town to restock."

"Can you please do something with that...that creature?" Owen asked, pointing at Harley.

Carson smiled at me. "Would you mind?"

Personally, I was okay with letting my dog terrorize the man for a little longer. "Not at all." I walked over and took the leash from Vincent, then knelt next to Harley. "It's okay, boy. He's not going anywhere." Harley stopped growling and butted my hand with his head. I giggled and picked him up, then returned to stand next to Delia.

"Before Carson locks you away, tell us why you hid the bag underneath the deck at the Bean." Vincent crossed his arms and gave Owen a threatening scowl.

"Yeah." Zoey placed her hands on her hips and took an intimidating step forward. "And why you tried to frame Archer for your crimes."

I'd already shared my theory with the rest of the group, but it would be nice to hear firsthand if I'd been right. Not to mention, a confession would most likely help Carson with his case.

"There's never anyone on the beach, and the lot for downtown shopping is usually empty that time of night, which is why I chose it to park my vehicle," Owen said. "I hadn't expected some teenagers to be partying on the beach." He ran his hand through the short strands along the side of his head. "Explaining my car would've been easy, but a bulky duffel bag, not so much. Stuffing it behind the panel seemed like a good idea at the time."

I remembered Archer asking Owen why he hadn't been to his place in a while. "That's why you were at the Bean the first time we met. You were checking to make sure the bag was still safe."

"Yes," Owen hissed through gritted teeth. "And I would've come back later and retrieved it if..."

"Harley and I hadn't already found it and turned it over to the police," I said.

A siren blared in the distance announcing that Carson's backup had arrived. Not long after that, Owen was told his rights, cuffed, and hauled off to jail.

Once the excitement was over, we all headed back to Vincent's place, so Myrna could get Ziggy, and I could get my car to drop Zoey at home, then head back to Delia's house.

"I wished we could have asked Owen how he picked his targets or knew so much about his victims," Delia said as she settled on one end of her couch with Luna perched next to her. "But I was afraid to push my luck with Carson."

I didn't blame her. Carson made sure to let everyone know before he left that they'd be having a discussion about what happened later. I didn't envy the lecture my aunt and her friends would no doubt receive. I was thankful that all I got was a directive to have a safe trip home and a reminder that he'd call if he had any questions.

"I have a theory about that," I said.

"You do?" Delia asked.

"Uh-huh." I kept a firm hold on Harley's squirming body so he'd stay in my lap and not disturb the cat. "Remember when we were at the Promenade's office, and Owen overheard our conversation?"

"Yeah."

"Well, I'd be willing to bet he spent quite a bit of his time eavesdropping."

Delia smirked. "People love to chat with Avery about their personal lives, so it wouldn't be hard for him to gather information."

"Or know who was attending an event and leaving their home empty," I said.

"It's too bad we can't prove it for certain." Delia ran her hand along Luna's back until she purred. "But I have a feeling Carson will eventually uncover the truth."

Thinking about the tenacious deputy made me smile and wonder what it would be like to observe one of his interrogations. "Of that, I have no doubt."

CHAPTER FOURTEEN

The excitement from the night before, coupled with the thought of having to leave, hadn't helped me get much sleep. Even cuddling with Harley hadn't been enough to relax me. I stared at the empty suitcase lying open on the guest bed, then at the pile of clothes stacked next to it. Clothes I'd been unwilling to pack for at least five minutes now. Thinking about the long drive ahead only seemed to make my procrastination worse.

Now that my vacation was almost over, I had to face the reality I'd come to Hawkins Harbor to escape. I'd been so caught up in solving a mystery that I hadn't made any attempt to find a new home for Harley. At least that's what I kept telling myself. If I were being honest, I'd grown attached to the little guy and really didn't want to give him up.

Keeping him with me meant taking him from his home and subjecting him to a colder climate, something I wasn't looking forward to either.

Career-wise, moving to Minnesota was supposed to be a good opportunity, so why did the idea gnaw at my stomach every time I thought about it? Maybe Delia was right. Perhaps it was time to follow a different path, one that only I was responsible for choosing. Exhilaration rippled through my system as thoughts of how I wanted to spend the rest of my day formulated in my mind.

Harley had been lying on the floor with his head on his front paws, watching me. Picking up on my excitement, he pushed to his feet and shuffled around me, tail wagging.

"Come on, boy," I said, snapping my fingers to get him to follow me down the stairs and into the kitchen.

Delia stood near the sink, staring through the window facing her backyard and the beach and ocean landscape beyond. She shifted away from the counter as soon as she heard us enter the room. "All ready to go?" she asked, sadness filling her voice. Her shoulders were slumped, and she appeared to be on the verge of tears.

"Not quite," I said, fighting the reactionary moisture filling my eyes. "Is that offer to stay with you for a while still available?"

"Yes, of course." She pulled me into a tight hug, then clasped the sides of my cheeks. "Why?"

"Can we talk about it later? There's something I need to do first." Harley whined and pawed my leg. "Sorry, but you're going to have to stay here."

"Do what you have to do," Delia said, smiling as if we had a psychic connection and she could read my mind. She bent down and snatched the dog off the floor. "I'm sure we can find something to do until you get back."

After kissing Delia's cheek and earning several licks from Harley in the process, I grabbed my purse and headed out the door. During the walk to the Bean, my anxiety had grown steadily stronger with each step. The emotion wasn't fear-based, nor was it derived from trepidation. I was excited about my decision and was looking forward to the upcoming negotiations.

It was early afternoon. The lunch crowd had dissipated, and only a handful of people sat at the tables on the deck. When I reached the bottom of the stairs, I placed my hand on the railing and took a calming breath.

My vacation might not have gone the way I'd envisioned, but it had provided some much-needed insight and a path to a fresh start and an adventurous future. With that in mind, I climbed the steps and went inside. As soon as I opened the door and spotted Archer working behind the counter, I smiled and said, "If you have the time, I'd like to discuss the position you have posted in the window."

* * *

ABOUT THE AUTHOR

Nola Robertson grew up in the Midwest and eventually migrated to a rural town in New Mexico, where she lives with her husband and three cats, all with unique personalities and a lot of attitude.

Though she started her author career writing paranormal and sci-fi romance, it didn't take long for her love of solving mysteries to have her writing cozies. When she's not busy working on her next DIY project or reading, she's plotting her next mystery adventure.

Made in the USA
Middletown, DE
30 December 2022